And Miles To Go Before I Sleep

Coach House Books acknowledges the financial support of the Government
of Canada. We are also grateful for generous assistance for our publishing
program from the Canada Council for the Arts and the Ontario Arts Council. Coach House Books also acknowledges the support of the Government
of Canada through the Canada Book Fund.

LIBRARY AND ARCHIVES CANADA CATALOGUING IN PUBLICATION

Title: And miles to go before I sleep / Jocelyne Saucier; translated by
Rhonda Mullins.
Other titles: À train perdu. English
Names: Saucier, Jocelyne, author. | Mullins, Rhonda, 1966- translator.
Description: Translation of: À train perdu.
Identifiers: Canadiana (print) 20210169478 | Canadiana (ebook)
20210169486 | ISBN 9781552454213 (softcover) | ISBN 9781770566644
(EPUB) | ISBN 9781770566651 (PDF)
Subjects: LCGFT: Novels.
Classification: LCC PS8587.A38633 A6213 2021 | DDC C843/.54—dc23

And Miles To Go Before I Sleep is available as an ebook: ISBN 978 1 77056
664 4 (EPUB), 978 1 77056 665 1 (PDF)

Purchase of the print version of this book entitles you to a free digital copy.
To claim your ebook of this title, please email sales@chbooks.com with
proof of purchase. (Coach House Books reserves the right to terminate the
free digital download offer at any time.)

And Miles To Go Before I Sleep

JOCELYNE SAUCIER
TRANSLATED BY RHONDA MULLINS

COACH HOUSE BOOKS, TORONTO

To the memory of Lise Pichette

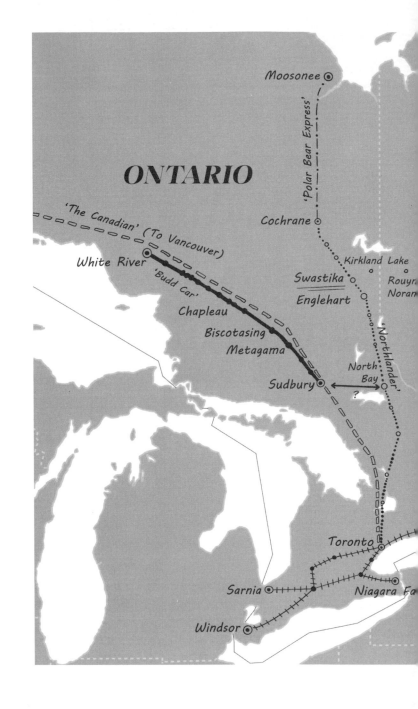

QUEBEC

Obedjiwan

Senneterre

Clova

Parent

Wemotaci

'The Transcontinental'

d'Or

Jonquière

Quebec City

Hervey Junction

'The Ocean'
(To Halifax)

Montreal

Ottawa

'The Corridor'

UNITED STATES

On September 24, 2012, Gladys Comeau climbed aboard the Northlander and was never again seen in Swastika, which is not even a town, not even a village, just a community along the railway line.

So began our journeys, both Gladys's and mine, because this is the tale of the travels of Gladys Comeau on the trains of Northern Ontario and Quebec, which took her south, then west, then east, then back north. An erratic journey that no one understood and that was tracked by many from the moment the old woman's disappearance was reported. There were many eyewitness accounts, opinions too; some pointed the finger at her, condemned her, called her a monster. My purpose here is not to put her on trial, but to follow Gladys on her frantic journey by train, to collect the scattered pieces and figure out what may have motivated her. Because while we now know about the detours and U-turns, the nomadic journey of the woman from Swastika, as she would come to be known, has been subject to many interpretations.

The shockwaves spread beyond her circle of friends and acquaintances, but there was nothing in the paper, there was no police investigation. When people in Swastika tried to alert the authorities, Gladys would reappear on another line, and another call would follow to another conductor. The affair remained private, there was no public attention. Who is going to take an interest in a woman who left her life behind, an ordinary woman, with no great feats or misdeeds to her credit, and old to boot? Me, it would seem, running counter to common sense and my own circumstances.

I don't have the heart of a tracker, any particular talent for investigation, or a penchant for mystery, and yet this story consumed me for more than four years. I retraced Gladys's journey, and I met scores of people who knew her or spent time with her before or during her travels, not to mention the calls, emails, and texts to inquire about departures or arrivals on a particular line, double-check a detail, chase down a name I had missed, that escaped me. I have file folders and megabytes filled with a story that leaks in every direction.

How did a man who was in no way destined for such an adventure end up wandering off into lives not his own? As I write this, I still wonder whether, as the son of a railwayman, I would have set out on the trail of an old woman if there hadn't been at the start a lonely station, a train whistle, and the promise of the rattle of the rails lulling Gladys and me, each on our own journey. It is hard to fathom the power of steel gliding over steel. It is familiar music that lives inside me. I admit to being a fan of trains, and that's what is behind me setting off on the trail of Gladys Comeau. But there isn't only Gladys; there are all the others who hailed, hounded, and hitched me to this quest or inquest – I don't know what it is anymore – that I now have to chronicle.

I have to explore, explain, understand my motivations.

But I will tell the tale, I will commit it to paper, I promised. Will you still be of this world when I will have finished this chronicle, Bernie my friend?

Swastika is not an easy place to leave. The village has a population of two hundred, tallies its residents one by one, every one of them counts, so a departure does not go unnoticed.

Gladys Comeau knew that, having lived there for the past fifty-five years, and she left the way you would mail a letter, the only way to leave Swastika. No suitcase, no new clothes, nothing to suggest a journey or departure, she walked down Avenue Conroy, hung a left on the government road, a right on Rue Cameron, then climbed the eighteen steps to the promontory on which the station is perched. She could have kept going, walked along the platform to the viaduct that straddles the government road, and no one would have been surprised to see her up there, since her morning walk often took her that way.

The platform of the station offers a view of the whole village. The roads winding through the hollows, the houses huddled together: it is all there in a panoramic view. From this higher ground, you can see the foam of the river as it arrives, follow the water along a park, and then, right before you'd end up back at your starting point, you can see a tiny church in the palest of blues perched on a slight elevation. Swastika has a particular brand of charm, a beauty that is easy to overlook. The station is not part of this aesthetic. It is an ugly brick rectangle that has seen better days, set along the embankment. Back then, the trains would arrive at all hours, as would taxis, trucks laden with gold bars – not even armoured trucks, not even tarped trucks, just trucks – in an endless flurry of activity, and the station was perched on its promontory, its grass lovingly maintained, forming a sort of skirt that descended to Rue Cameron, and, at the centre of its skirt, in red, yellow, and a symphony of colour, begonias, pansies, and marigolds, forming a huge swastika.

There is no grass anymore, nor other attempts at preening. The windows have been boarded up, and the station is closed except for one room that serves as the waiting area, deserted except in bitter cold, because there are no creature comforts, not even bathrooms, and people prefer to wait on the platform.

And on the platform that chilly September morning, there were two men and one woman, which pleased the conductor, because often there was no one, and he had to continue on his way. Gladys was a regular on the Northlander. The conductor, one Sydney Adams, recognized her immediately.

I say *conductor* knowing full well that the word is no longer used in the administrative jargon of the railway. In Ontario and Quebec, they are now called *service managers*, the railway employees who greet customers, see to their comfort, ensure everyone gets off at the right stop and that their luggage gets off with them. I have always known them as conductors, and that is what they will remain during this tale.

But I digress.

I imagine this story will be punctuated with digressions, flashbacks, personal notes, and other asides. I have a considerable amount of information, and I have to extract what is most credible in the accounts I've gathered over the years. Mostly vague, uncertain accounts, fragmented because they concern a disjointed journey that no one witnessed from beginning to end. Some parts are better documented, for instance the stops along the Sudbury–White River line, because these were stops with people she knew, long-time friends, 'children of the forest,' as she called them, who are as nostalgic as she is for a bygone age. They are the children of the school train, charmed children from a charmed time, friends from her childhood, the happiest days of her life. In the interviews they granted me, you can see where Gladys's irrepressible optimism comes from, how she got along with life despite the setbacks, her refusal to hold a grudge against it. 'When you have known happiness, it's impossible to believe that it's no longer possible.' It was one of the things she liked to say.

The friends who were her neighbours painted the same picture: an eternally optimistic woman, determined to be happy, who didn't buckle where many would have fallen. Some had known her since she moved to Swastika, a young bride head over heels in love, and who formed, with other neighbourhood friends from Avenue Conroy, Avenue Childs, and Rue Westinghouse, a community of support. Some ten people, including Frank Smarz, one of my most trusted allies in this investigation. He is central to the dogged pursuit that began the moment Gladys's disappearance was reported.

Frank Smarz (fifty-five years old, welder by trade, and a blueberry- and dandelion-wine buff) is the husband of Brenda, Gladys's next-door neighbour and close friend, or at least she thought so until that morning in September when her friend left Swastika without breathing a word of her intentions. More than anyone else, she was devastated by Gladys's disappearance and, while she doesn't want to admit it, she was deeply hurt not to have been in on the secret. I had to contact her several times before she agreed to tell me her version of the story of Gladys's disappearance. The other members of the community weren't so reticent.

A *community of support* is the perfect term to describe the neighbourhood friends – ten at most, people of modest means – who over the years developed an easy, open friendship; even they are astonished at how naturally it happened.

They have each other over for dinner, help each other out with home repairs, swap tools and clothes (just the women) but never money – an unspoken rule among them, no loans. And if there is the odd hiccup – if there are words, moods, or behaviours that wound, frustrate, or hurt – they let the bad times go by just as surely as the good; time is their surest ally – except in this particular case.

Gladys was a frequent beneficiary of this friendship. Having been widowed one year after moving to Swastika (a mining accident, common at the time), she raised a daughter on her own, a daughter who was her pride and joy, until one day she found her in a pool of blood, her first suicide attempt. Lisana was twenty at the time, a pretty young woman, a nursing student, smart, cheerful, light-hearted; she was everything you could want in a child you pampered, coddled, moulded with care and love. Gladys was devastated. But she never gave up hope. Her optimistic nature led her to believe that it was a crisis that would pass, a bump in the road of life. She never stopped hoping for better days. Not when she got the second call from the nursing school, not the times she had to go pick up Lisana in Toronto, from a squat, a shelter, a hospital room, and when she brought her back to Avenue Conroy, cared for her, pampered her, then watched her leave, hoping she would never again have to hear a stranger's voice on the phone telling her that her daughter had given in to her urge to die. The people around her were driven to distraction watching her struggle. Lisana had been resurrected, but for how long? How long before she relapsed? How long would it take for Gladys to understand that there would be no end to it all? Or that there was only one possible end … but no one dared think about that, let alone say it.

Her neighbourhood friends had nothing but good things to say about Gladys. A courageous woman, extraordinary, a devoted mother, a protective mother, a mother who did the impossible. The epithets gushed forth, admiring, full of praise. But when it came to Lisana, people would shake their heads, looking like they had a lot to say, and you would have to guess at the despair and bitterness behind their dark faces. A lot of blame was laid at Lisana's door. If it had been up to them, they would have left her to her fate long ago. But no one said so.

These are people who are wary of their feelings and emotions. The only thing I ever managed to get out of them was facts. During the four years I travelled regularly to Swastika, I felt they trusted me but never considered me a close friend. If they have a secret garden, and everyone does, they tend to it away from prying eyes, maybe even away from their own awareness. Living in such a tight-knit community for so long, you end up forgetting about yourself. But facts, on the other hand, reign supreme. They can be rehashed, burnished, stored a long time in memory, and if a stranger comes knocking at your door, facts can be pulled from their treasure chest and put on display. So I got a detailed, in-depth account of the day Gladys disappeared, leaving behind her one Lisana, whom they wanted nothing to do with.

It was Brenda Smarz who raised the alarm. Homes are transparent in such a small community; one lives out in the open, and all it took to start Brenda's worrying was to notice that Gladys's bedroom curtains hadn't been pulled back in the morning. At 11:15, unable to contain herself any longer, she decided to go check. She knocked – no answer – then went in and crept as far as the kitchen, where she spotted Lisana at the table with a coffee in front of her, sitting erect, stock still in her chair, entranced by an invisible point on the wall. It scared her.

Lisana was hardly a young woman anymore. She was fifty-four, but she looked much older, having been so broken by a life she was bent on destroying. 'She looks her mother's age,' people always said. They went on about her grey complexion, absent look, shuffling gait, 'as if she has the weight of the world on her shoulders.' The feelings she still inspires in them made the picture they painted all the darker. To hear them tell it, mother and daughter had nothing in common. And yet, they will still say, when you would see them walking down the streets of Swastika, both high-waisted and big-boned, you could almost mistake one for the other. The look of Scandinavians, with blond hair and pale, almost milky blue eyes, but in Lisana's case, everything was covered in ash, no radiance, whereas Gladys, they were careful to point out, had always taken pains with her appearance. Hair cut in layers, dyed to its original blond with a home kit, complexion brought out with light makeup. 'Beauty is for everyone,' she was fond of saying, and while she stopped dyeing her hair and wearing makeup in her late sixties, she wore the marks of time with discreet and elegant resignation. No one would have pitied the old woman she had become if it had not been for Lisana, always at her side, wherever she went, casting a shadow over the pair they formed.

So Lisana 'had a black flame burning inside her' when Brenda approached her, a hard, vicious glow that made her unrecognizable. 'I thought she was in crisis.'

Brenda had never seen Lisana in crisis. That is another reason she was angry with her friend. Gladys protected her daughter to the point of hiding her from view when a difficult patch loomed. That's what she called it, a difficult patch, a bad spell; it was all she would say after shutting herself away with her daughter, for days, sometimes a week, not leaving the house, to hide the marks of the battle they waged. *Lisana has had a bad turn*, was all she would say. Brenda knew better than to ask her any more. 'She was as exhausted as if she had given birth to Lisana a second time, but chatty as ever; she talked about her flowers, a joint of meat she was going to roast, things around the house, as if she had just returned from a trip and had resumed her daily routine, but about what she had gone through with her daughter, not one word, not even to me who told her my whole life story.' And she sunk into a sulky silence.

So Lisana had a black flame burning inside her, and Brenda got scared. She believed that a crisis was coming, or the ravages were already being felt. She ran room to room searching for Gladys, fearing the worst, and, not finding her, went back to Lisana. She asked where her mother was, and Lisana slowly turned from the point on the wall she was staring at and said, 'Gone,' smiling a smile that would make your blood run cold, a smile as terrified as Brenda herself was, standing before this stone woman, and Brenda flew out of there, leaving Lisana, who had not moved from her chair, absorbed by the horrible smile that had crept over her face.

It took no more than fifteen minutes for word to spread. 'Where is Gladys?' They looked everywhere; the entire community mobilized. They went up and down every street, checked the park, walked along the river, searched Gladys's house top to bottom, again questioned Lisana, who had relaxed her hideous smile but was of no use because she just kept repeating, 'She's gone – She won't be back – She's gone,' in an endless litany that ultimately had to be believed because Gladys was nowhere to be found.

At the Smarzes', where the neighbourhood friends gathered, speculation was running rampant. It was also at the Smartzes' that people would gather in the days that followed and make calls to improbable train lines to try and find Gladys and bring her back to Avenue Conroy. Their house would become command central for her *repatriation* (the word they used). But for the time being, they were in shock, completely baffled, trying to understand. What was most incomprehensible, most inconceivable, is that Gladys had dumped Lisana on them.

They knew they had lost precious time trying to understand why Gladys had done what she had done. They did the math: had they not gotten bogged down in pointless questioning, they realized, Frank Smarz's call to the Englehart dispatcher would have been made well before noon and would have been relayed in time for the conductor to intercept Gladys. That was not their only misstep. Time kept playing against them, often a matter of minutes, wrong route, poor timing, she had just left or had gone in another direction – their messages never managed to get where they were supposed to, when they were supposed to. They felt as though their timing was off from the beginning: 'All that time, Gladys's Toyota was sitting there, in front of our eyes, in front of her house, so it was clear she had taken the train.'

It was 1:30 when Frank Smarz phoned the Englehart dispatcher. It took the dispatcher a while to understand ('more minutes ticking by'). He sent the message by radio to the conductor of the Northlander, Sydney Adams, who confirmed that Gladys had boarded at Swastika, but he had no more to say because there had been a crew change in North Bay. The conductor who took over in North Bay was Edward Murphy. When he received the message, Edward Murphy had just noticed, in checking his documents, that he was missing a passenger.

This message would be relayed from train to train over more than 3,000 kilometres without anyone being able to stop the course of time. Gladys was covering her tracks. Whether it was deliberate or not, they still wonder.

Conductors are important witnesses. They make the same trip year in and year out, and they often know their passengers by their first names, regulars who board and disembark in a small town, a village like Swastika, or a clearing in the forest. They are in the heat of the travel action, and they are stones to be turned over to trace Gladys's journey.

The first stone to be turned is Sydney Adams, conductor on the Northlander. A number of conductors will make an appearance in this tale, but Sydney Adams will be the first – as chronology demands – even though I only met him two years after these events.

At the time, he was in forced retirement, the Cochrane–Toronto line having been eliminated on September 28, 2012, four days after Gladys was spotted on it. The Northlander and Gladys Comeau disappeared almost at the same time. Some believed it was a cruel twist of fate. Indeed, it seems that the tracks of destiny opened and shut in perfect synchronicity for Gladys to continue her getaway.

Sydney Adams's wife had taken advantage of her husband's retirement to plan long trips to Florida until, unable to stand any more sun, golden beaches, or daiquiris, the husband fled the idleness that was weighing on him. He was a workhorse, as he liked to say, a man who believed that life's salvation is in work, wherever it can be found. So he had built a relatively prosperous life from his job on the rails and what he called his hobby (houses he bought, lived in, renovated, and sold at a profit – one that was 'reasonable', he took pains to point out; 'I'm not a money-grubber').

The meeting took place at his home in Cochrane, a house that was a construction site, walls knocked down to create an open space ('It's what people like these days'). His wife, a scurrying little mouse, kept darting between the construction area and the tea and little cakes throughout our conversation.

He was surprised to learn that anyone was still interested in the story and somewhat reluctant to tell what little he knew. He blamed himself for not realizing what was happening on board and for letting Gladys slip away. But sitting there for two hours, with no riveter or nail gun in his hands, nothing to do but chat, he was even more talkative than I had hoped. I know men who are so locked in their thoughts that they don't know themselves or what torments them. With too many cares about today, the next hour, right now, they don't let thought disrupt the series of tasks to accomplish. A hard-working life doesn't lend itself to introspection or outpourings. During our conversation, they were few moments when Sydney Adams indulged in personal reflection.

He is a man cut from one piece, not very tall but stocky, with bushy eyebrows and a piercing gaze, and he radiates an energy focused on the present moment. In this he is like my father, my uncles, all the men of my childhood. *Train men*, they used to say among themselves, as did Sydney Adams. His voice had the smell of sludge, the hammering of tools, the heavy gait of the giants of my childhood, coming and going between the trains in our station in Senneterre. I was in familiar territory.

When he realized that I too was a lover of trains, the conversation took a turn. I was treated to stories of the glory days of the Northlander and to hardy 'buddy's, which he would have punctuated with just as hardy and friendly claps to the shoulder if I hadn't been out of reach in my armchair.

'Gladys loved trains too,' he told me. Despite their lack of comfort, their slowness, their unreliability, and the fact that almost no one depended on them anymore. 'Gladys was born on the train, in fact, a long time ago. She was seventy years old, but she was still strong, strong enough to make the trip on our trains. Always with her daughter, Lisana, the poor thing.'

He had known them for as long as he could remember. During the glory days of the Northlander, they were often on board. They went to Toronto, to Montreal, had travelled to Nova Scotia, to Winnipeg; they had seen almost all of Canada by train. Lisana, as a little girl, and then a little older, colouring in her colouring book, reading romances, while her mother went seat to seat, chatting, laughing, kidding around. Then there were the incidents that Sydney Adams couldn't explain ('such a sweet kid, so cheerful'), and Gladys would bring *the poor thing* back from Toronto. Lisana would watch the scenery go by while her mother, spilling over with cheer, would try to drag out of her even just a glance. In those moments, Sydney Adams sometimes took the time for a bit of the conversation Gladys's daughter wouldn't offer her.

He liked having Gladys aboard. 'She was chatty; she could talk about anything and everything for hours.' It is a long trip from Swastika to Toronto. You have to allow around ten hours, not counting the delays, which were many, because freight trains take priority over passenger trains, which regularly have to pull into a siding. Having on board someone like Gladys, who goes seat to seat and livens things up, as if the car were a village street, was a blessing for both the passengers and for the conductor.

But on her last trip on the Northlander, not a word, not a move, 'didn't even go to the bathroom.' She sat there with her nose glued to the window the whole trip.

He might have worried, but his attention had drifted to 'the man with the scarf,' which he said with a sidelong glance, knowing I too was from the North. We were compatriots, so to speak.

'It's not like I haven't seen plenty of weirdos on the train.'

That's what he blames himself for. Letting himself be so distracted by the weirdo that he forgot Gladys. Even on the platform, waiting for the Northlander with Gladys and another traveller, the man had intrigued him. It was the scarf that caught his attention, although it was not particularly remarkable, 'a striped grey scarf.' And I offered up the little laugh he expected. A scarf is an unusual affectation for a Northern man, something a bit laughable that does not pass unnoticed.

'A stranger, I thought. Not someone from around here.' (And I was treated to another heartfelt 'buddy').

So two men and one woman were waiting for the Northlander that September morning. The stranger in the scarf who would absorb his attention, and a second traveller squatting near a canvas bag and Gladys. Sydney Adams immediately recognized the second traveller: he had been on board just two days before. 'A Ukrainian who spoke nothing but Ukrainian. I don't know how he had managed to get around without a word of English.' As for Gladys, he recognized her immediately but was surprised to see her without her daughter.

My quest had long moved beyond factual reconstruction when I met Sydney Adams. I had already gathered enough information to piece together Gladys's itinerary. I had moved on to wondering about her motivations, about what she knew of her own intentions when she climbed aboard the Northlander.

Did she give the impression of a woman on the run or on a suicide mission?

'Gladys wasn't in the mood to talk that morning.'

She barely offered a perfunctory *thank you* when he helped her aboard. She went to her seat without greeting the other passengers. Then, nothing. She didn't move from her seat. As still as a stone. He wasn't terribly surprised. He figured Lisana had run off and Gladys had to go get her yet again. If he had taken the time, he would have wondered about Gladys's behaviour, because it had been a long time since she had had to drag her daughter back from the under-belly of Toronto – years, in fact – but his attention had already drifted to the man with the scarf.

'A weirdo … For a while I thought he was a train buff.'

Sydney Adams wasn't speaking a foreign language. I know train buffs. They are fanatical about trains. They ride the rails of the world in search of an old locomotive still in service, a line that is on its last wheels; they take huge risks for a photo of a trestle bridge from below, venture where they are unwelcome just to check the year a locomotive or a caboose was made. They are American, European, Australian – not a woman among them. For conductors, they are a nuisance or a source of amusement, depending on whether they are meddlesome or entertaining.

When the Northlander was still running, it connected to the Polar Bear Express, a northern line that runs from Cochrane to the shores of James Bay, the land of the Cree, and because of this, it attracted its share of enthusiasts. Tourists, journalists asking a lot of questions, anthropologists who had sometimes come from far away, and, from time to time, a train buff who had also come from far away with a list of questions. Sydney Adams thought for a moment that the man in the scarf was one of them. But there was too much refinement in his manner of dress (the scarf, a well-cut jacket, and a saffron yellow shirt … saffron yellow!) and no questions about the Northlander, the Polar Bear Express, or the Cree community of James Bay.

'But asking questions, yes. Bothering everyone with his goddamn questions.'

He had met a lot of passengers, and they all had bad things to say about him. The man was nervous, jumpy, intrusive, irritating, a pain. He kept going from passenger to passenger the whole trip. It wasn't his manner of dress that was off-putting, or the way he had of bending over you as if he were going to shower you in compliments ('any more polite, and he'd have to erase himself from the planet'), but rather his insistent questions, which inevitably went unanswered, because no one knew the Trotsky to whom he referred.

They had nothing to say about Gladys, except that she didn't move from her seat and didn't have any luggage.

There weren't that many of them, ten at the most, gathered in a single car, the Northlander not being what it used to be. It was a chugging milk-run train, just three cars long (passengers, baggage, and snack bar), that drew only people who enjoy a leisurely pace, its swaying, the squeal of steel on steel, the whistles of a powerful beast, and those who have no choice but to go slow.

In addition to the three passengers who came aboard at Swastika, there was a mother with her three young children; a young Cree man from Moosonee; a few seniors, mainly women; a welder who was heading to a job in North Bay; and a retiree from the Ontario Northland Railway, who as such got to travel for free. While he didn't know all the passengers by name, Sydney Adams knows how to spot the purpose of a trip. In the case of the old women, no need to overthink it, they were going to visit family or see a doctor in Toronto. They had with them a soft-sided cooler, to save money or because they didn't trust the food in the snack bar. Others also had a cooler and had already started unwrapping sandwiches when Sydney Adams saw the man with the questions sidle toward the seat of the young Cree man.

'Indigenous people keep to themselves.' They travel as if they were still in the forest, silent, hushed. Even in groups sitting in double-facing seats, they can make the whole trip without exchanging a word. Sydney Adams, convinced the questioner would come up against age-old Indigenous stolidity, watched the man's manoeuvring.

That's when Gladys got away from him, or at least that's what he thinks.

'We were coming into North Bay, and she probably slipped into the gangway connection while I was watching what would happen next.'

What happened next was curious. As he had previously done with the other travellers, the man bent over the young Cree man (no more than twenty, according to Sydney Adams) and spoke to him at length. To the conductor's great surprise, the young man's face lit up; he almost smiled. The stranger felt permitted to sit down near him, and they started a conversation that Sydney Adams, try as he might, couldn't hear from where he was.

'I was blown away. I had never seen anything like it. Normally the Cree don't let themselves be bamboozled by someone who talks a good game.'

This explains why he didn't see Gladys get off the train in North Bay. He was so busy watching what was going on that he got behind in his work, and his passengers were already getting off, helped by the relief crew that was waiting on the platform.

'I wouldn't have let her leave like that, without a word, if it hadn't been for that damn guy with all the questions.'

An unfortunate series of events. Things had taken a bad turn. Gladys had given her pursuers the slip, and somewhere, someone was filled with regret.

The name of the damn guy with all the questions was Léonard Mostin. He is French and a writer but was thought to be a Jewish historian, red herrings that meant it took me a while to track him down. My story already has its share of digressions and departures, so I won't get into how I managed to find him on Rue de l'Éperon in Paris.

I set out on the man's trail because of his inquisitiveness. I knew from Sydney Adams that he had had no contact with Gladys on the Northlander, except for a quick look as he passed by her to pester passengers with unwanted questions. But alone with her on the platform (leaving aside the other traveller, the Ukrainian who spoke only Ukrainian), hadn't he had ample time to ask her where she was going and what she was going to do there? Who knows what she might have told him. I was banking on the man's insatiable curiosity and on the conversations people sometimes have with fellow travellers.

Léonard Mostin is indeed a prolific asker of questions. The man I met in his tiny Paris apartment jibed in every respect with the picture that had been painted of him. Jumpy, nervous, fidgety, and churning with questions. But not intrusive, not a muckraker, nothing unpleasant. Quite the contrary. He had a deep, sincere desire to reach out to others in order to escape, I thought, his own inner agitation. He wanted to know everything about me. Where I was from, what I did there, whether I was happy there, and how many more years I would spend in my little town before I would grow weary of it.

He knew what had brought me to see him. We had met on Facebook and kept in touch via email. But he was finding it hard to understand how he came to be associated with something that in no way concerned him and of which he knew very little when we met in his little mouse hole (I can't imagine living in such cramped quarters) in Paris.

He definitely remembered Gladys. It was the absence of luggage that piqued his curiosity. 'All she had was a bag on her shoulder, not a purse, more like a tote bag.' And her immobility. 'She was staring blankly, not making the slightest gesture, motionless in a dense shadow, as if she didn't belong to this world.'

'Gladys. Is that really her name?'

His English was limited, minimal, but good enough to be surprised at such a cheerful name for a woman who to him seemed so sombre and uncommunicative. His French, on the other hand, was lively and bubbly, like champagne. I never got tired of hearing it. He made no comment on mine.

I can easily imagine the thousand and one questions that emerged from this man in search of the humanity of others when he saw this older woman who, like him and the other traveller, was there for the 09:40 train. But he told me she wasn't moving, like a statue, with no luggage, and she never looked in the direction the train would be coming from. He approached her, greeted her with a nod. 'Nothing, she didn't move, didn't even look at me.' He grew bolder, offering the most charming hello he could, 'and still, nothing, not a word, as if I didn't exist.' He didn't insist, moved along the platform, and his thoughts got lost in the foaming of the river.

He too was lost, as he tried to explain, involved in a quest that consumed him.

'My thoughts deserted me as quickly as they came to me.'

It was an elegant way of saying that he felt completely lost in this village at the end of the earth where he found himself alone and without bearings among people who were almost openly mocking him.

He spent four days in Swastika on a quest that makes mine look perfectly reasonable.

Léonard Mostin is not a man for travel. Born in Paris, he has spent years in the same apartment in the 6ᵉ Arrondissement. The little cafés on Rue Buci, the large bookstores on Boulevard Saint-Germain, the street life, the chance encounters, the fellow writers, the publishers wandering along Rue Saint-André-des-Arts, Rue de Seine, Rue Mazarine, a bustle particular to Paris that kept him from looking any further. And all it took was one word, just one, entered in Google, for him to cross the Atlantic.

It was in googling the word *swastika* that he discovered that there existed, lost in the great Canadian expanse, a place that had 'the impudence – the heedlessness – the arrogance' to go by such a name and, even more impudent-heedless-arrogant, to fight to keep it. The battle of the Swastikans was reported in detail on Google, along with their battle cry: *To hell with Hitler; it was our name first.*

I too searched on Google, and I felt the same scandalized surprise when I read the story that came up on several sites.

In 1940, there was a sign war in Swastika. At the time, the name had the stench of blood and destruction, and the Ontario government wanted to change it to the name of the celebrated cigar smoker who was waging war against horror in Europe. But for the people of Swastika, their place name was good luck. The community had been established with that name decades earlier around the Swastika Gold Mine. And for months, Winston and Swastika were at war at the village limits, signs ripped out, then planted again, then ripped out again, until the government retreated from its engagement with the local army. *To hell with Hitler: it was our swastika first.*

It was this unbelievable story that prompted a Parisian homebody to make the long trip to lose himself in the wide-open spaces of the Canadian North.

'I wondered whether the people were either idiots or committed pranksters. You have to be nuts to defend the swastika these days.'

If he had thought it was just an idiotic prank, Léonard Mostin wouldn't have set out on the adventure.

'The truth is I was bored with my novels. I couldn't stand my own writing anymore. My fifth novel was going to be as stuffy as the previous ones, and I was suffocating with anxiety at the idea of shuffling around in it for years because I had nothing else to do.'

So he left in search of some sort of epiphany that might await him at the end of the world in a community of jokers or lunatics who took pleasure in perverting history. He would find a novel ripe for the picking, funny and forceful, an impressive lark; not knowing what direction it would take nor how it would end, he would be kept in suspense in his little apartment on Rue de l'Éperon.

Léonard Mostin did not go unnoticed in Swastika or in Kirkland Lake, the neighbouring town where he was staying. People still remember him clearly; they told me about him in amused disdain. A string bean walking the streets with a hesitant step and asking a string of questions of anything that didn't move. Swastika, obviously, was what interested him, the origin of the name and what people thought of it, and he left with little more than that 'Swas' was a great place to live. I got essentially the same answers when I questioned the people of Swastika.

Swas. Not once did he hear them utter the word *Swastika*, only the diminutive. He concluded that their unconscious held some shame. But the word came back, the whole word, crisp and resonant, when he ventured to ask whether they would take up the sign war again if required. 'Swastika is our name.' That was the answer, and it was offered with the hint of a challenge.

Pride in the swastika had indeed existed. There were still traces of it in the amused smiles his questions were met with, but the townsfolk had no intention of letting anyone root around in a collective unconscious that belonged to them and them alone. Léonard Mostin was used to witty conversationalists in cafés, not people of few words who let silence say the rest. He would trip over his awkward English when he tried to get more out of them.

Pride and shame, strange bedfellows. There was a novel in it, but how would he find it if they kept blocking his path. His plans were unravelling, appearing increasingly nonsensical, and every evening he would find himself in his cold, faceless little room wondering what he was doing there. He would have left a lot sooner if he hadn't met Bernie Jaworsky at the municipal museum in Kirkland Lake. That's when his unformed project changed course.

I have come now to my friend Bernie, to whom I owe my understanding of the foolishness of any fictionalization and who was the driving force behind this chronicle.

Bernie Jaworsky, seventy years old, maybe older, a retired teacher, a historian in his spare time, and my most faithful companion on this journey. Despite the age difference, we got along as if we had always known each other. There is something in us that vibrates at the same frequency. I thought it was because we were both teachers, biology for him and English for me, he at the high school in Kirkland Lake and I at the comprehensive in Senneterre. But there's a lot more to it than our occupation, a lot more than this investigation Bernie has followed from a distance. There is a little note that I hear in him and that he must hear as well. We have the same emotional tone, a little disjointed, a little remote; in that we are alike. I call him and he immediately knows what's going on, whether I'm having doubts, whether I'm lost in the morass of accumulated information, or whether I simply need to hear my voice in his.

I met him at the Kirkland Lake municipal museum. He's almost always there. Bernie is a local history buff. He published *Lamps Forever Lit*, a book about fatal accidents that occurred from 1914 to 1996 in the mining camp at Kirkland Lake, which includes the mines in Virginiatown, Matachewan, and Swastika, and many more. The accident that took Albert Comeau, Gladys's husband, is included, described through the strict objectivity of facts. No emotion in the description of the fatal fall, no outrage at the absence of security at the mine, no finger pointing, no calls for justice or reparations. Bernie Jaworsky stuck to the unflinching reality of facts. It is this refusal to let himself be carried away by emotion that makes him an invaluable ally. A great deal of aimlessness was avoided thanks to his keen sense of reality.

In fact, he described Léonard Mostin this way: 'That man has no common sense.'

Léonard Mostin had also wound up at the municipal museum. It seems the roads of all travellers meet there. At the museum, they thought he was a Jewish historian, because of his interest in the swastika. There, as elsewhere, his eager questioning soon started bothering the museum's volunteers, who out of desperation turned to Bernie, also a volunteer at the museum and the last-ditch reference for lost causes.

Bernie is a serious man, hard-working, conscientious, a man who dedicated his life to work and family, not one given to fun and games. He appreciates a good joke, but it would never occur to him to make one. When you see a smile dance on his lips, you know he has thought of something funny and that he is hesitant, doesn't dare, wonders whether, and in the end keeps the story to himself.

I saw the smile doing its little dance. He pressed his lips together to hold in what was funny, and then, no longer able to contain himself, went for it.

'The man looked like a child waiting for Santa, he had put so much hope in me. I knew this would take hours. There was no way I could let him be scandalized by a name that has made its place here and that doesn't deserve all the fuss being made of it. So I did my spiel about the swastika: its Neolithic origins; its cosmic dimension in the East; its modern meaning; Coca-Cola, which used it in its advertising; Lindbergh, who had it on the hub of his propeller; and the Swastika Gold Mine, which had been our good fortune long before Hitler hijacked the symbol. I ended with the words I always use in these sorts of situations. 'We have a sense of history, but we also have a sense of our history.' I could see it wasn't enough, that I needed something else, that he needed a riddle to solve, a shadowy corner, a cantilever to tip. So I told him a story that I've never believed but that made the rounds at some point here, and that some people believed.'

The story is deliciously mischievous, and it is incredible that anyone believed it. It said that Leon Trotsky spent three weeks in this back of beyond, walking the streets of Swastika and Kirkland Lake, notebook in hand, jotting down his observations about the living conditions of miners. In spring 1917, right before the Bolshevik Revolution.

Hoaxes don't stand up to historical fact for long. Léonard Mostin realized this in reading Trotsky's autobiography once he got home. Which I also read, and in which I found no trace of the celebrated revolutionary in Northern Ontario.

This hoax is just Swastikans thumbing their noses at anyone who doubted their existence up there in their village. And yet there were people who believed it. I even saw it on the official website of the city of Kirkland Lake. Then it disappeared from the site; people eventually no longer believed it or were secretly ashamed.

Léonard Mostin, who had believed it, was not at all offended or ashamed at having been duped. When I met him in his mouse hole, he was having a grand old time with a novel that combined war, love, betrayal, vengeance, redemption, and Indigenous legends in a country at the end of the earth, where people were stricken with a strange illness that rendered them mute; it featured Hitler, Churchill, Trotsky, a young Cree man in love with a flowery young white woman, an old woman who carried death within her, and a Ukrainian who had come to spit on his grandfather's grave.

Bernie's comment: 'He probably should have stuck to the story about the Ukrainian.'

He doesn't like the idea of a story that blends fact and fiction. He's afraid that people he has known for a long time, friends or neighbours, will find themselves twisted or caricatured in it; he's afraid he will be too, disguised or, worse, under his own name; he doesn't trust the imagination of a man who does not have a firm footing in reality; he thinks that what he told him about the Ukrainian is worth more than any of his foolish imaginings and that Gladys never, ever carried death within her.

On this point, he is intractable. Gladys does not deserve to be portrayed that way. Yes, death paid a violent visit fifty years ago when her husband fell at the Lake Shore Mine, and it was a constant presence during all those years when her daughter slashed her wrists over and over again. But, and he insisted on this point, Gladys did not carry death within her.

Bernie is not close to Gladys. He saw her from time to time when she came to run errands in Kirkland Lake, said hello to her the way you do in small towns where everyone knows each other without really knowing each other, was vaguely aware of her story before really delving into it for his book.

Bernie met with her twice for the entry about her husband, and even though both times it was about the circumstances surrounding her husband's accident, at no point did death weigh heavily in the conversation. On the contrary. He told me that 'she was much more interested in sharing her small pleasures than cataloguing her sorrows.'

'Her small pleasures?'

'Trinkets, plaques, figurines, macramé, the house was full of them, a real candy jar.'

Gladys was living good years, it seemed to him. He met with her at her home, and he could see how she took care of it. A house full of flowers, both inside and out, a nicely arranged deck in the back, frilly curtains in the windows, sunny watercolours on the wall, glass beadwork mobiles, and other trinkets she made herself. She had been living with her daughter for years at that point. The daughter didn't say a word to him when he arrived or when he left, just stared at the TV, headphones in her ears, never looking toward the kitchen, where the conversation was taking place. Lisana seemed calm and clearly absent, shut away in her world, 'practically to the point of being autistic,' but absolutely not the mad, threatening woman the neighbours had described to me.

He had all the information he needed to write up Albert Comeau's entry, except for the names of the pallbearers at the funeral. The entries sometimes got into these minor details. The book covers 310 fatal accidents over a period of eighty-two years. It took him four years, a long and fastidious piece of work, almost obsessive in its precision. Each entry briefly introduces the miner (nationality, previous employment, etc.), describes the operations that led to the accident and the injuries that were the cause of death, provides the results of the investigation, and ends with the funeral and the burial.

Research for Albert Comeau's entry was almost complete. In fact, he had a first draft. Working at Lake Shore Mine for just one year, Albert Comeau had fallen from the top of a sixty-foot raise climber. He was killed instantly (cervical fracture), and the death was certified by Dr. Marvin Casey. The investigation concluded it was an accident. The funeral took place at St. Pius Church in Swastika, and he was buried at the Kirkland Lake cemetery. All he was missing was the names of the pallbearers.

Aside from this missing information, the point of his visit to Gladys was to check his draft, three tightly condensed pages. She read it and reread it slowly and earnestly, lingering on a word, coming back to it, spreading the sheets before her, smoothing them with her hand, caressing them, then, with a weary smile in which you could read all the years lived without her beloved, she spoke these words: 'My Albert will be much better off in a book than in a cemetery.'

'Gladys didn't carry death within her; she was a mountain of will and energy, a monument to life.'

And he burst into tears.

'I'm the one who has carried too many deaths, too many deaths for too long.'

Then he calmed down.

'Don't let him do it. Don't let that crackpot mix our lives up in with whatever hare-brained things he invents. Take notes so you don't forget anything, don't overlook anything, because one day you will have to write this story.'

I promised, I wrote everything down, recorded everything, saved everything, and I now find myself with a story that takes off in every direction. Too many facts gathered, too many anecdotes collected, too much of everything. A massive forest to clear. If one day there are readers for this story, may they forgive me the mess. Because I'm only at the beginning, and I can already feel the dangling threads.

Bernie my friend, I have too much stuff. How do you contain the ebb and flow of the ocean?

Recorded here anecdotally and extraneous to this chronicle, the story of Stefan Malinowsky, as told by Bernie Jaworsky.

'I don't know how he managed to make the trip without speaking anything but Ukrainian. All I know is that he was staying at the Super 8 motel, that he showed my book to the woman at the front desk of the motel, saying my name and repeating it until she decided to call me. When I arrived, he opened the book and pointed to the entry for Wasil Malinowsky, better known here as William Maloney.'

Bernie is of Ukrainian origin, and he managed, with what remains of his mother tongue, to understand that the man was the grandson of this Wasil Malinowsky, and that he was most humbly asking his help to find his grandfather's grave. He was a man of around fifty, solidly built, stocky, with a crewcut and features like someone with Down syndrome, having given little thought to his clothes, humble but determined. Bernie was impressed that a man would come from so far and after so many years to visit the grave of a grandfather he clearly didn't know. According to the entry in *Lamps Forever Lit*, Wasil Malinowsky, who died in 1948 at the Chesterville mine, had left his native Bukovina in 1931, well before the birth of a string of grandchildren in the Carpathian Mountains.

Stefan Malinowsky had gone to the cemetery the night before and couldn't find his grandfather's grave. And for good reason. It was an unmarked grave, without even a flat grave marker bearing the name of the deceased. But Bernie had no trouble finding William Maloney's grave. He was a regular at the cemetery, his book having taken him there often. He still returns to honour his dead, to honour the living who come to put flowers on the graves of their dead, and he has a detailed map that allows him to move between the cemetery plots as confidently as through the streets of his town.

Wasil Malinowsky aka William Maloney was resting beneath his rectangle of grass, forgotten by everyone but this man who had made the journey to bring him the respects of his family so far way. Bernie stood at a respectful distance but was close enough to hear the astonishing things the grandson said to his grandfather.

'I am the son of Zenovia Holubec and Josef Malinowsky, the son you never held in your arms, never looked upon with your eyes, brother of Nikola and Yawdoha, the children of Baba, my grandmother, which makes me your grandson, and I do not bring you my respects. I have come to give you news of your family, who do not send their respects, who wish you all the ill you deserve, that you may now be suffering the torment that Satan reserves for his creatures, that is what we all wish you in memory of Baba, our sweet, gentle Baba, the cousin you married, put to work, impregnated three times, abandoned on the third to follow your friend Alex Susla, who was going to find his fortune in Canada, because you didn't want a third child with a flat face. Admit that you fled our flat faces, that you fled the scorn of the villagers, that you fled like a scoundrel, and once you arrived in Canada, you changed your name, you took up with a village woman, that you had four healthy children with her, whom you raised like a good father should, while we in Lekechi passed on the gene in the most abject poverty and universal contempt until I arrived, me, your grandson, almost free of the curse. Years later, the granddaughter of your friend Alex Susla came to get to know the land of her ancestors and told us the whole story and left us the book that enabled me to come stand on your head and spit on you. Here, Grandfather, is the spit of Baba, Nikola, Yawdoha, Joseph, your grandchildren, and your great-grandchildren, who are many and without a defect among them.'

The man was speaking in a monotone voice, without emotion. Bernie felt like he was attending a ceremony with a long-established ritual. The man was officiating calmly and solemnly. Once the speech to the dead man was done, he thoroughly cleared his throat and forcefully projected a thick, long snake of spit onto the grass. Bernie shivered (in disgust or astonishment, he doesn't know). But the ceremony was not at an end, because the man, with the body language of an officiant, unzipped his fly and soaked the perimeter of the rectangle of grass.

The outrage toward the deceased was spent, which Bernie sensed in how the man's shoulders slumped – his entire body, in fact. In the cold breeze of that fall day, the man was teetering with fatigue. Bernie softly approached him and, without a word, they left the cemetery.

Bernie drove him back to his motel. It is a few kilometres from the cemetery to downtown Kirkland Lake. The man, slumped in the seat, was silent, lost in thought. When they arrived at the motel, he recovered his spirits and, remembering his manners, thanked Bernie and bid him farewell. He was leaving the next morning for the long journey home. Bernie offered to drive him to the station the next day, but he declined under the pretext that he had already reserved a taxi, which only added to the mystery of the Ukrainian travelling in Ukrainian.

Bernie often comes back to this story, to the fact that he didn't drive the Ukrainian to the Swastika station, which he regrets terribly because he thinks if he had, things would have been different. He would have run into Gladys, could have kept her there, prevented her from getting lost on the rails. It is a feeling shared by everyone directly or indirectly connected with Gladys. They feel responsible for a word, a gesture, a look that they had or didn't have, lost forevermore in the series of missed chances that allowed Gladys to wander off on her own.

At the top of the list of misfires is Frank Smarz, who didn't go to Sudbury. He still blames himself for it. 'If I had gone to Sudbury, I would have put an end to all this before it even got started.'

Frank Smarz is a man of action. He is not satisfied with assumptions and suppositions. And that is what he won't forgive himself for. For having deluded himself.

First misfire, first derailment in a chase that would see its share.

When they learned that Gladys had gotten off the train in North Bay, they could reasonably conclude that she then took the bus to Sudbury. Because Gladys's sister Elizabeth lived in Sudbury. Her parents had died long ago, her two brothers were somewhere in Australia or Asia, so the only one left was her youngest sister.

'Think, think, that's all we did. What's the point of racking your brains with nothing but air?'

Air, to Frank Smarz's way of thinking, is the conversations, the illusions they create, the time wasted getting tangled up in them, and for the first few days of Gladys's disappearance, everyone convinced themselves that she had just gone on a trip.

That's what the sister from Sudbury had told them on the phone. Gladys had slept over at her place and the next morning had taken the train for Chapleau. She had simply decided then, as she sometimes did, to retrace the route of the school train, to go back to the landscape of her childhood. A trip that would take a few days, a week at the most, the sister had said.

In Swastika they breathed a sigh of relief. They were no longer thinking in terms of a disappearance, but rather a trip, which contained within it the idea of a return. Gladys would come back to them with her joyous smile and would talk about this and that, which would bring back other memories that she would recount again and again. There was no end to the marvellous tales of the life she had lived on the school train.

Days would pass as they awaited her return, and Frank Smarz would gnash his teeth.

'If I had got in my pickup, if I had driven for four hours, just four hours, I would have been there way before she left for Chapleau, and I would have put a stop to all this.'

Two years later, I went to Elizabeth Campbell's. Frank Smarz grumbles whenever I tell him about it. But she didn't tell me anything we didn't already know. It is the fact that I did what he never did that ticks him off.

I had no particular expectations when I knocked on Elizabeth Campbell's door. I had been warned. Gladys was as talkative as her sister was not. And indeed, when she opened her door to me, I felt I hit a wall of silence.

The conversation was short, barely an hour. I have never felt the absurdity of my situation more. What was I doing there, five hundred kilometres from home, sitting across from this wordless woman, asking questions to which I already knew the answers?

I wanted to see her, Elizabeth Campbell, Gladys's younger sister, whom I had seen only in pictures. I had been told that Elizabeth was a carbon copy of her sister, a younger, less likeable version. But that's not enough to justify the five hundred kilometres.

And yet it is. I know that now. They are the kilometres that took me away from my little town and back and that kept me on the move for four years. It is hard to fathom the pull of a small town. When you are born there, when you have your family, your friends, and your habits there and it isn't enough anymore, it takes more strength than I have to leave. My lack of courage is why I am still in Senneterre, alone, single, and childless, limping from I don't know how many love affairs. Having always wanted something else without knowing what it was, I had the opportunity to set off in pursuit of a story that kept running off ahead of me and gave me the illusion of movement. I thought I had become a great traveller. I came and I went, always on the move, hundreds of kilometres that maintained the illusion until I found myself back in my bungalow, my old armchair, and the desire to sink into it. The great homebody traveller.

An old woman had the courage to leave her village one fall morning and, even if only in the form of a younger, less cheerful sister, I wanted to see her. I had no other reason to knock on Elizabeth Campbell's door.

She might have had all the features to create a face that looked like Gladys's. A high forehead, well-defined eyebrows, eyes that appeared to be milky blue but that you had to make out underneath the drooping eyelids, broad cheekbones that opened up her face, all covered with a layer of wrinkles and suffused with a profound melancholy. I was looking at the image of a Gladys who was older, it seemed to me, than the one I was chasing.

When she walked ahead of me down the hallway to the living room, and I saw her use her hands to help move her stiff legs forward like timbers, I understood the melancholy that emanated from her. She was immobile, a prisoner in this house, alone for too long, and she had lost her taste for others.

She had succinct, uninteresting answers to my questions about Gladys's impromptu visit the evening of September 24. Gladys had arrived tired, with a cold, and she had taken the train to Chapleau the next morning. All of which I already knew. The conversation had barely begun, and I had just exhausted it. A heavy discomfort, a keen sense that my presence was unwanted.

What followed was a strange conversation. Me trying to break the silence with questions about Chapleau, Gladys's trip, the school train, and her sinking into her thoughts, not paying attention to me, as if I weren't there. I had hoped to bring her around with memories of the school train, anecdotes. But it was clear that the topic was way inside, deeply buried, and only came out in stray phrases in a long stream uttered with a sigh. 'The clatter of the rails ... large cypress and small larch ... the clatter of the rails in the marrow of our bones ... large cypress and small larch ... in the sharp curve of Metagama ... they wait for us ... dreams, desires deep in our guts ... coming, going, pitching, dancing ... slowly ... large cypress and small larch wave hello ... should we make a wish?... close your eyes ... after small larch ... after Metagama ... your most intimate wish ...'

She fell asleep in her armchair, legs resting ramrod straight on the cushion on the coffee table, and on her lips, the tiniest trace of an inner smile.

Back to Frank Smarz. Of all the neighbourhood friends, he was the most useful in reconstructing Gladys's erratic itinerary. He was also the one who told me about what was happening at Gladys's house while she was train hopping. He was her next-door neighbour, her go-to man, the one she called when there was a heating or plumbing problem, something major; she wouldn't have bothered him with a leaky faucet. Frank Smarz knows Gladys's house as well as he knows his own.

In fact, this was always how he approached Gladys. 'Everything okay at home?' They would talk pipes, windows, heating, but never about Lisana, even though he knew the main problem in that house was Lisana, whom Gladys protected with every fibre of her being against the slightest dirty look, the merest word that might slip out and disrupt the delicate balance at home.

Frank Smarz never knew the little girl brimming with intelligence or the dreamy teenager. He met Lisana in her mid-thirties when he moved in with Brenda to the house next door. Lisana was already there, having moved back in with her mother a year earlier. She was their age, but had too much life experience, had taken too many nosedives, had too many breathtaking rebounds, and she seemed decades older than them. They had only ever been her mother's friends.

The other neighbourhood friends, on the other hand, remember the good years. Gladys and Lisana, blond and laughing, coming home from the school where Gladys taught and Lisana learned. Gladys and Lisana picnicking in the park. Gladys and Lisana in the swing in the backyard. Gladys and Lisana making puppets at the kitchen table. Their laughter and their handiwork were what the neighbours remembered most and what they wanted to share with me. They couldn't understand how a child so radiant could fade so completely overnight.

I got to know these people. There was a time when I spent almost every weekend in Swastika. I was won over by the friendship of the neighbours, a scarce, precious resource, which they are aware of and tend to. A friendship shared equally, a community friendship – they speak in a single voice. (I see from my notes that after a certain amount of time with them, I no longer bothered to identify who was speaking. It is the choral voice of the neighbourhood friends I have reproduced here. Except in the case of Frank Smarz, to whom I owe the strict accuracy of facts – we spent hours bent over maps and train schedules – and his wife, Brenda, because of the special friendship she thought she had with Gladys.)

It happened overnight; that's what they couldn't fathom. Lisana was studying nursing, a model student, a beautiful young woman, and overnight she foundered, became unrecognizable.

When Lisana moved back in with her mother, they didn't understand that either. She needed to settle, to forget about things, Gladys tried to explain. As the weeks, months, and years went by, they grew accustomed to the presence that made the air feel heavy and sucked all the oxygen from the room. 'If you let her look you deep in the eyes, you won't have a minute of peace.' All they could do was escape, and that's what they did, each in their own way; they turned their backs on her to avoid being unsettled.

The two women lived together fairly peacefully for twenty years. Gladys had retired and collected more small pleasures around her daughter. Not once was there an ambulance on the hill on Avenue Conroy. People started to believe in the possibility of redemption. She still had her difficult moments, periods of crisis when the neighbours wouldn't see either of them and would watch from afar, counting the days. They were used to it, just as they were used to the vagaries of the weather, to snowstorms that leave in their wake a heap of scenery to shovel, comment on, size up, telling yourself that, in the end, this one was better or worse, that thank god Gladys had made an appearance again, exhausted, a bit haggard, but out of the house, and there were no more marks on Lisana's wrists. You can get used to anything, even death lurking, and the neighbourhood friends who maybe secretly hoped for the act that would free Gladys from her burden were clearly no less relieved when the storm had passed.

Lisana was unconcerned about the dark faces, the way they had of speaking to her distantly, as if she weren't there and they weren't there either.

'Disconnected from herself,' Brenda said.

'Completely shut down,' her husband would say less delicately.

When Frank Smarz has to say more than is strictly necessary, he is at a loss. You can sense his exasperation, mired in the words that come and go in his head; he tosses his head in helplessness and then it comes out, brutally, furiously, bearing no resemblance to what he wanted to say.

The day after Gladys left, many of the neighbours went to knock on her door. Which Lisana cracked open long enough to say, 'Don't need anyone,' closing it immediately, then locking it. She couldn't stand to see them at her door. Brenda was reduced to watching for the movement of the curtains. Morning and night, she would see them open and close in Lisana's bedroom. Nothing else moved. For a few days, only Frank Smarz was permitted entry, and then once he was turned away, he had only the phone to ensure there was no irreparable harm happening behind the closed door. Bizarrely, Lisana answered; she didn't refuse his calls or those of the others who besieged her by phone.

When he went in the first time, he asked her, 'Everything okay in the house?' as a way of reminding Gladys's daughter he was the go-to man, that he had authority in this house. And she answered, 'It's more than I can bear.'

Frank Smarz thought that it was taking care of the house that was more than she could bear, while Lisana was expressing her complete inability to live. A profound misunderstanding.

So he went through the rooms to make sure everything was as it should be, relieved to have to check the taps rather than spend any more time with Lisana.

'A power surge' is how he describes Lisana. 'She was 25,000 volts, at least.' A power surge, but contained in cold immobility. When he returned, she hadn't moved from where he had left her. 'Everything is all right. You don't need to worry,' and he had already opened the door, ready to leave, when he remembered that he had come to give her news about Gladys. 'Your mother took the bus to Sudbury. She'll be back soon.' Lisana didn't move, didn't bat an eye, an oracle in the living room.

He came back in the days that would follow under different pretexts. He would bring her meals that Brenda or another neighbour had prepared. Lisana, with the same intensity, the same immobility, had not a word of thanks for the neighbour, only the words that expressed her inability to live, but that he understood otherwise, and Frank Smarz did his rounds of the house again to see that everything was as it should be, that the meals hadn't been thrown in the garbage (he checked), and would quickly get away from her.

'What wasn't right in the house was the silence.'

It took time for it to dawn on him. While he went from room to room searching for the sound of water running or a draft that would give him cause for concern, he was so relieved to get away from Lisana that he didn't realize what was actually haunting the house. It was only after having told this story and many others that it occurred to him what was missing in Gladys's house: the television, the soaps, the noisy game shows, the explosions, and the jingles, the mishmash of sound that assailed you as soon as you went through the door. Because there wasn't just the television in the living room; there was the radio in the kitchen, the television in Lisana's bedroom that she would forget to turn off. No matter what time you showed up, the house was shouting, throbbing, yelling from all sides. It was so bad that Frank Smarz came to believe without really believing that Gladys wanted to escape the noise in her house. Without really believing, because who would leave their life behind for such a silly reason?

Four days went by that way, on hold, waiting, for Gladys to come back 'with the feeling that we were missing something.'

On the fourth day, they got a call that gave them hope they could hang on to. Suzan Sheldon, a school train alum and friend of Gladys's, called from Metagama. The connection wasn't very good; Frank Smarz could barely pick up a few words, but got enough to understand that Gladys had just left Metagama and that she was on her way to Chapleau. There could be no further doubt; Gladys had heeded the call of nostalgia and was retracing the route of her beloved school train.

The school train. We have finally arrived. There was not just Gladys's nostalgia; there was my own fascination. I was struck, utterly, by the school trains, a head-on collision with major damage, a fascination that kept me in a state of alertness around anything to do with them. To the point of sometimes forgetting about Gladys and getting lost down sideroads.

Gladys was born on a school train, and she lived on one for sixteen wonderful years, the daughter of William Campbell, a travelling teacher who taught her about all the possibility a day holds and the sun that always ends up shining. Gladys had a happy childhood, happier than any child in the world could dream of, a dedicated childhood, a childhood that had meaning and significance, a childhood like no other, and she returned to it every time she was in danger of foundering. To truly know Gladys, you have to know about her childhood, the years of pure happiness when she took in what she needed, not to be later swept away by Lisana's dark waters. 'When you have known happiness, it's impossible to believe that it's no longer possible.'

The school trains are no more. Few people know about their existence. What I know comes from the old-timers, former students I met along my own journey. I searched the internet, the libraries, municipal museums (almost every small town in Northern Ontario has one), and I didn't find much, a few pictures and information riddled with holes. I visited the rail museums in Saint-Constant and Capreol to see a replica of an old school train. I read, cover to cover, *The Bell and the Book* by Andrew Donald Clement, a travelling teacher who put in twenty-seven years on the school trains. But the former students were the most useful. They told me piles of stories. I will try to record here only what is necessary for understanding Gladys and her journey. But I don't make any promises, because my fascination tends to sprawl and could splash onto the pages.

So here it is.

From 1926 to 1967, seven school trains cut across Northern Ontario to bring the alphabet, mental math, and the capitals of Europe to children of the forest. Seven school cars, seven schools on wheels, as they were also called. Set up as classrooms (desks, a teacher's lectern, blackboards, bookshelves, everything to accommodate twelve students and their teacher), the cars were basically mobile schools. A freight train would pull the car over a distance of around twenty kilometres, leave it on a siding, in the middle of the forest, from which emerged a group of children who for a few days would learn reading, writing, and arithmetic, a bit of history and geography, until another train came to pick up the car and take it twenty more kilometres, to where other children awaited it. The mobile school made five, six, or seven stops along a one- or two-hundred-kilometre line and returned a month later to the children at the first stop, who had waited all that time with homework and lessons. The stops corresponded to the tiny villages where trackmen maintained the track and kept trains supplied with water and coal (it was the era of steam locomotives). This was how education was dispensed, a few days at a time, to not only the children of the trackmen, but also to all those who lived in the surrounding forest, the children of prospectors, woodsmen, trappers, Indigenous people, and fire wardens. Wild little children of the forest, most of whom on their first day of school had never opened a book or uttered a word of English, being the sons and daughters of immigrants, Cree, or Ojibwe. Some of them did their ten years of schooling, some pursued their education elsewhere, becoming nurses or engineers, but all of them cherish the memory of that car that brought to them the wonders of a world to discover, both in books and in the train itself. It's something they still talk about with awe: the linoleum on the floor, the varnished maple panelling, the curtains on the windows, the flush toilet, the battery-powered radio, the oil lamps – it all gleamed with opulence and novelty in the eyes of children of the forest.

The teacher had his quarters on the train. Three tiny rooms with the modern comforts of the times: a kitchen, a bathroom, and a central space that, depending on the hour, served as a sitting room, dining room, or bedroom. The little Campbell household was home to four children, a dog, a cat, and a skunk they had tamed and that then left them for no reason, as well as the many visitors that their extraordinary presence on the train attracted. Life was exhilarating, fascinating, thrilling, exciting, always in motion, a perpetual merry-go-round. The Campbell children grew up with the swaying of the train and the feeling that their parents were humanity's benefactors. Gladys more than any of them because, as the eldest, she helped her father in the classroom with the little ones and her mother in the family home. Her mother who, in addition to her household tasks (which were no doubt many), helped women write letters or fill out a list for orders at Eaton's or provided care for sick children.

The school train was much more than a school. It was where they offered evening classes for adults (reading, writing, counting, and Canadian democratic institutions for immigrants), medical care and vaccinations (a doctor came twice a year), bingo nights, radio evenings (particularly during the war). They welcomed hoboes for hot meals during the Great Depression, children in makeshift beds on blizzardy nights, and an entire small community on its own for Christmas. Gladys often talked about how much fun they had making decorations and trimming the tree with the children on the school train. Fun that would wane as the stops went by, to be completely depleted by the time they had to organize their own family Christmas in Chapleau. After each stop, she would say, laughing, they threw the tree and the decorations out the window and started over at the next stop.

Life on the school train was made up of these pleasures and these labours. Gladys maintained a strong predilection for the swaying of the train, time without end, the trees, lakes, and rivers that slowly streamed by, and the cool smell of resin that greeted her when she got off the train in one of the forest hamlets that stubbornly continued their uncertain existence, where she would find a child of the forest who had grown as old as she had.

But there was no nostalgic escape in the journey Gladys had taken this time. Suzan Sheldon can testify to that, as Gladys had stayed overnight at her house in Metagama, a ghost settlement lost along the Sudbury–White River line (just a few houses, no sign announcing their presence).

So now I've come to Suzan, a child of the school train, close friend of Gladys, the only one she truly confided in. (Brenda, her friend in Swastika, got only a few crumbs; she knows it and she chews on them bitterly.) But Gladys confided nothing during her last visit with Suzan. Gladys arrived in the rain, with no luggage and no Lisana. Suzan thought that the tragedy that had been a long time coming had finally occurred, that Gladys had come to digest her sorrow at Suzan's. But Lisana was fine, Gladys said. The two women have known each other for too long to make each other believe in lies. They spent two days together talking only about little memories and the rain that wouldn't stop. Not a word about whatever had brought Gladys to Metagama without warning, and that seemed to weigh a ton. Unlike the others who found themselves on Gladys's route and who languished in guilt, Suzan regretted nothing of what wasn't said. She is convinced that she wouldn't have been able to change Gladys's mind. 'Behind her eyes, behind what she refused to tell me, it was the same old Gladys, determined, wilful Gladys, convinced she was on the right path, and no one, absolutely no one, could have diverted her from it.' But she still grabbed the phone as soon as Gladys left.

Metagama is accessible only by train. To get Suzan's account, I had to retrace Gladys's journey on the Budd Car. This is what they call the self-propelled car that makes the trip from Sudbury to White River. The Budd Car crosses flat, even bleak, countryside, plenty of peatland and stunted forests, nothing grand enough to move the soul of a traveller, but fortunately, here and there, graceful distractions: the shimmering of a lake wreathed in foam or of a river the train runs alongside for a moment, that is lost and found again, cool and crystalline. You have to be from the North to appreciate the austere beauty.

The Budd Car travels west on Tuesdays, Thursdays, and Saturdays and returns east on Wednesdays, Fridays, and Sundays. I arrived on a Tuesday, so I had to wait until Thursday to return to Chapleau, where I was going to meet other former pupils of the school trains.

This meant that my conversations with Suzan took place over the course of two days. I slept in the bed where Gladys had slept on her last visit. 'We didn't even sleep together,' Suzan told me going into the bedroom in a tone that was meant to suggest how strange the last visit was. She had to explain it to me. This bedroom belonged to her son, Desmond, who came to see her every weekend. It was also Lisana's when she accompanied her mother to Metagama. As for the two old friends, they shared a bed, a habit that lingered from the years on the school train.

Suzan was the daughter of the head trackman in Metagama, and because she was the youngest in a long line of children (there were six of them) often left to their own devices because of a sickly mother, she was regularly cared for by the Campbell family, who all but adopted her. So she was an addition to the four Campbell children, and she shared their nomadic lifestyle, for which she has nothing but praise and admiration, as well as sharing Gladys's bed, where they spent long hours talking. 'When one of us finally fell asleep, the other would move so we were lying head to toe, because otherwise the bed was too narrow to sleep.' And she laughs – she is quick to laugh, always ready to burst. 'If you sleep with feet in your face, you will never be under the weather.' Suzan also had things she liked to say.

They slept together whenever Gladys came with Lisana to spend a few days. Like the two sisters they could have been, and were, when all is said and done, they had so much in common. Both with a ready laugh, tall, and thickset (they traded clothes), a happy childhood they liked to think back on, and the same worries. They both had a child who had reached age fifty without becoming self-sufficient. Lisana, who had no appetite for life, and Desmond, struck very young by what his mother called 'the malady of words' and who had nothing but that in his head, 'the poem he wrote, the poem he is going to write, the poem that won't be written,' all of which left his pockets empty. Her son lived and still lives in Sudbury, where he earned his living from small carpentry jobs and whatever his mother gave him to sell. To help her 'handyman poet' (no sarcasm on Suzan's part, just a twinge of sadness infused with amusement), she started doing handicrafts. Mittens and ushankas made from old woollen garments, second-hand clothing her son brought her from Sudbury on the Saturday Budd Car, along with her groceries for the week. He made himself useful, repaired the generator, cleared snow off the roof, built stores of firewood, and went back home on Sunday afternoon. It is an arrangement that suited them both.

But – and there is a but, and not a minor one – the two women's children couldn't stand each other. As soon as they were in the same room, they would turn their backs on one another. 'As if they were the like poles of two magnets,' Suzan sighed when the conversation got to that point. (Desmond, whom I met at a Tim Hortons in Sudbury, had another explanation: 'I couldn't stand the way she looked at me. There was something in her that struck a nerve. I couldn't tell you what it was. A huge void, or a vortex. It would take me days and a lot of work to extract myself from it.')

So Gladys avoided the weekends. She would arrive with Lisana two or three times a year, loaded up with provisions, new clothes (for Suzan), and used clothes (for her mittens and ushankas), and would spend a few peaceful days in the little house under the trees.

Suzan's house is indeed as calm as they come. All you can hear is the rustling of the leaves and the chirping of the birds. It is the old house of the head trackman, her father, which she and her husband fixed up into a four-season cottage and which she has lived in alone since her husband's death twenty years ago.

A terrible racket took over Suzan's peaceful, solitary house every time a train passed. When one did, it was impossible to hear each other speak, and you had to stop any conversation. Suzan would stop rocking in her rocking chair, attentive to the noise and the vibration that seized the house, and once silence was restored, would say 'fifty-nine' or 'seventy-two' or 'eighty-seven' – cars; she had counted them!

Aside from the Budd Car, there were around ten freight trains that passed by Suzan's door, and every time, I would see her counting the cars in her head.

A childhood game, a game played by children of track-men driven mad with solitude in the immensity of the forest and that still amuses the old woman she has become: Clickety-Clack.

'It's the sound the wheels of the cars make at the junction of rails. Two series of wheels at either end of the car, so two clickety-clacks per car. You have to add up the clickety-clacks and then divide by two to get the total number of cars.'

It was our first evening together when she explained the clickety-clacks to me. I had arrived at her house in the after-noon with my big bag. You don't just show up at the home of someone who is isolated without bringing your share of provisions, and I had way more than was needed to feed me for two days. Cheese, jam, salami, treats, and a few nice bottles of wine, without knowing whether she preferred red or white, because Suzan communicates with the outside world by satellite phone, and sometimes it is impossible to hear each other, particularly in bad weather. It took me days of torturous calls to make the arrangements to show up at her place.

I played Clickety-Clack with her, and I understood how fun it could be. It was zen. The sound is so powerful that it drowns out everything fluttering around in your head. You no longer belong to the order of thought when a train goes by; it transports you to a place where you never go otherwise. But I couldn't get the count right. I would say sixty-two, and she would say fifty-eight, and I knew from her smile that she had won.

The nostalgia of the train, the nostalgia of the whistle of those powerful beasts that awaken what lies in wait deep down inside us – was that what brought her back to this place in the middle of nowhere?

'It could be worse. I could be living in a condo with a view of the wall across the way or in a condo association meeting or being boiled in chlorine in a pool in Florida.'

A bit of footwork. She didn't want to answer the question. Or didn't have an answer to a question that was no longer asked of her, since she had grown so accustomed to this life. But I insisted. She had lived in Toronto, Calgary, and Vancouver, had held different jobs, had had an active life, was a woman of her times and then, once she was widowed and retired, she had found nothing better to do than to come back here (I almost said: to this godforsaken place) to listen to the passing trains and count their cars?

'Clickety-Clack isn't just a game of solitaire. I played it with Gladys too. When she came to Metagama, we would play Clickety-Clack, and she would win every time.'

But of course. Gladys played Clickety-Clack, and she won with the same subdued but victorious smile. It was hardly a surprise. Gladys is the queen in all the stories of the former school train pupils, and she is the daughter of the venerated William Campbell (not a negative word was ever said about him), who invented the game in anticipation of the trains that would pass close to the school train ('Practically grazed,' Suzan said. 'We were just feet from the main track, and it was a terrible racket every time; we couldn't hear each other speak, and Mr. Campbell would always have prepared mental calculations for us'). Mr. Campbell, always in a suit and tie, even in the middle of the forest. Decorum, order, discipline, and fervour. Every morning he would raise the Union Jack at the back of the car to greet the wild children of the woods. Washed, hair brushed and braided, and in their best clothes, they were also dressed up in honour of the day of school. They numbered seven, eight, twelve, sometimes only three or four. Some of them were just learning the alphabet, others could list all the prime ministers since Confederation; some had just arrived from Ukraine or Yugoslavia, others had never seen anything but the forest where they were born. It was a mixed-grade, multi-ethnic class, with a teacher mindful of each one of them. On the blackboard, on the left, the schoolwork for the day was listed by grade, and on the right, mental math exercises awaited the passing of trains. Addition, subtraction, division, multiplication, and, for those who weren't ready for such things, the little ones, a semicircle with two dots on top, the smiley of today's emoticons, communicating their duty to stay quiet during the clickety-clacks.

'And it worked, it worked like a charm on the school train. No strap, no dunce cap, no need for discipline, we were all so happy to be there! The older kids added, subtracted, multiplied, and divided, while the little ones, not a move, not a word, all smiles, eyes wide open, let themselves be carried off by the trains.'

And Suzan then added, which greatly surprised me: 'Like Lisana, when she would see us stop rocking in our chairs. She would take off her headphones and wait for the train with us.'

'Headphones. She had headphones?'

I remembered the episode of the headphones in Bernie's story: Gladys talking to him at the kitchen table while Lisana, headphones on, was riveted to the TV in the living room. I was intrigued by the headphones, by the fact that this woman people said was lifeless, apathetic – 'disconnected from herself,' as Brenda had said – could be interested in television and now trains, the clickety-clacks.

'The poor girl couldn't do without them. She wouldn't have lasted an hour without her horrible music. I wouldn't be surprised if she kept her headphones on to sleep.'

'She counted the cars too?'

'No, what she wanted was noise. It's incredible the decibels that poor girl needs in her head. She needs noise, a lot of noise, a deafening din that keeps her far away, far far away, in a world that doesn't need her to be here, there, or anywhere. All she wants is to be absent from herself.'

It was almost refreshing to hear it. Madness, mental illness, no matter what you call a disturbance of the brain or the liberties it takes, it all creates distance, and I only ever heard hesitant, cautious words about Lisana, words that were afraid of their own shadow.

Suzan wasn't afraid of Lisana. She had known her as a small child, had held her on her lap, had seen her crash at the cusp of adulthood, and had accepted it without worrying about the prickly person she had become.

'But what good are trinkets when you have lost the will to live, I ask you?'

She was referring to Gladys's small pleasures.

'That's the best she could come up with after the psychiatrists and psychologists came and went without giving her back her daughter. She threw the Prozac and the other stuff in the garbage and fought on the only battlefield she knew. Happiness. Pleasures big and small, particularly small. Happiness was her medication.'

Suzan was the only one who cast a critical eye on Gladys, the only one to openly express doubts about her stubborn attempts to keep her daughter on the sunny side of life.

'I ask you again, what good is birdsong when you wake up wanting to die? That was the cross Lisana bore every day. Opening her eyes and discovering that another day awaited her. You should have seen Gladys fight every morning to convince her to get on with a new day.'

Suzan had witnessed the long negotiations. Every time it was the same war of attrition between mother and daughter. Gladys had to argue for Lisana to agree to get out of bed, creep to the table, eat something, submit to the first acts of the morning that would get her to the end of the day.

'Lisana would say that she couldn't do it, that it was more than she could bear, and Gladys, calm and patient as always, would explain that the first step was the hardest, and that the rest took care of itself. And then, indeed, after a halting start, the rest wasn't so bad.'

People felt sorry for Gladys, for the hardship her daughter put her through. They railed against Lisana as much as they complained about how blind Gladys was, even though, according to Suzan, there were moments of closeness between the two women, moments when they leaned on each other, when they found the balance that had held them together for all these years.

Suzan had a sense of those moments when the mother and daughter would exchange a look after a train went by or on certain stormy nights. Lisana loved claps of thunder, lightning, the furor that took over the sky, and Gladys, sitting by her side, would watch the storm go by with her daughter, as if it were a carnival parade.

'There was a depraved joy in Lisana's eyes, whereas in Gladys's there was the twinkle of a flame. Who drew the other into whose world? It was hard to say. But after the storm, there was the same contentment in their eyes, the same relief.'

During Gladys's last visit to Metagama, there was a moment when it seemed as though Gladys was waiting for the storm with Lisana. It was her second night there, and the rain was coming down in sheets. Alarmed by something strange in her house, Suzan got up and spotted Gladys sitting in the rocking chair and, beside her, the other chair, empty, rocking.

'I could have sworn Lisana was there, beside her, in the chair that was rocking all on its own.'

There was no Clickety-Clack during Gladys's last visit, nor any long conversations. Nothing could distract her from what had brought her to Metagama and that she refused to say. They 'hadn't even slept in the same bed.' And yet these were their favourite moments, the long hours spent fending off sleep by rehashing old memories and their worries for their children.

Suzan believed and still does that Gladys never intended to stop in Metagama, that her visit wasn't really a visit, that she was forced to because of the fatigue from travelling.

'She was in a pitiful state. At first I thought she had a bad cold, then I thought it was the beginnings of pneumonia, she looked so bad.'

Gladys left Metagama on the fourth day of her rail journey with a travel bag Suzan had given her, filled with warm clothes.

Direction: Chapleau. It was the only one possible, because it was Thursday.

'You're too old for foolishness.'

That was all Suzan managed to get out as a goodbye.

The rain was torrential, and they were clumsily holding umbrellas. For once the Budd Car was on time, and Neil McNeil, the conductor, hustled Gladys onto the train to get her out of the rain. Suzan asked Neil McNeil, whom she knows well, who is a friend of sorts, to seat Gladys far from the drafts, and then she ran through the rain and straight to the phone, convinced of the urgency of the situation without knowing why.

Her first call was to the Ménards, Ronnie and Marta, both former pupils of the school train who now live in Chapleau. She wanted them to intercept Gladys if by chance she had intended to continue on to White River.

The second call was to Lisana. Suzan took a moment to think before dialling the number. She didn't know what state she would find her in, didn't know whether Lisana would speak to her, whether she would hang up or pepper her with insults (it had happened before) or her usual complaints. She went with a casual approach: 'Hello, Lisana, it's Suzan. Is it raining there?' – (…) – 'I'm asking because it's raining cats and dogs here, and your mother has just taken the Budd Car to Chapleau. Did you know?' – (…) – 'She's not in great shape, and I was wondering … ' and then, nothing. The line went dead. She doesn't know whether Lisana hung up or whether her satellite phone had died because of the storm. The line was crackling, spitting, it was unbearable at times, but she is convinced that Lisana was on the line; she could hear her breathing between the bursts of static.

Then she phoned the Smarzes, or at least tried. There was a terrible rumbling on the line. She did, however, manage to make intelligible the words she was yelling at the top of her lungs and that Frank understood, because she heard him shouting his head off at the other end of the line.

It was the beginning of many, many phone calls.

A few more words about Suzan. At this stage in the story, she is the one with the best clues to follow Gladys through the labyrinth of her race or her escape or her mission; none of it is clear so far.

It was the last evening for Suzan and me, in the little house under the trees. The air was mild, a train had just gone by, the house was settling after the clatter, and probably because I was going to leave the next day and an imminent departure draws out last confidences, she told me what she had thus far held back. A sentence that rang like a bell. A sentence uttered by Gladys.

'That child bathed in my tears.'

It was something that came to her the first time she found Lisana in a pool of blood, words that kept haunting her, a painful, obsessive mantra that she had repeated only to Suzan.

'That child bathed in the tears I didn't shed when Albert died.'

According to Suzan, that was the source of her immense guilt, her stubbornness, her refusal to surrender Lisana to anyone else's care, her support in anything that could keep the crises at bay, a life dedicated to her daughter: everything, absolutely everything, according to Suzan, came from the tears she refused to shed when her husband died.

Albert Comeau died in the Lake Shore Mine accident in 1958. There is nothing remarkable about that: miners died all the time, misfortune regarded as inevitable and endured in silence in order to not add to the terror that spread through the mining village with each accident. The terror of the miner who would refuse to work his shift. The terror of the wife who would stop her husband from working his shift. The general terror that no one spoke of so that life could go on. Hence the silence. An accident at the mine was never discussed, in private or in the street.

Gladys did what was expected of her and lived through her sorrow, holding firmly to the bastion of her silent tears, a courage she bitterly reproached herself for because – and it takes a mother to feed on such an obsession, according to Suzan – she believed the tears that swam in her belly had contaminated the unborn child. Gladys never wanted to explain her daughter's impulse for suicide in any other way.

Suzan obviously rejects the explanation. People are not destined for suicide before they are even born. Suicide isn't encoded in our genes. She could have added that suicide had become a way of life for Lisana, that the poor girl had made it a life preserver that kept her afloat through her dark waters, that the very idea of ending it gave her the strength to carry on, but these weren't things Gladys could hear. Nothing could convince her that this was not her responsibility to shoulder.

I didn't go back to Metagama. The trip is long and complicated, and I had too much to do to go down the rabbit hole of connections between Northern trains that get you there and bring you back on a schedule that suits them. I stayed in touch with Suzan. But we never again spoke about what she had confided in me on that last evening in the privacy of her little home.

My friend Bernie was the only one I could talk about it to. Bernie repeated the sentence in one tone and then another, as one would heft and weigh something being explored with the hands. We were in his basement, a cozy room where he is surrounded by everything that has been his life, photos, books, trophies from his soccer days, and in this snug atmosphere of a retiree's basement, he let the words sound in his head before making this comment: 'Gladys thought she was strong enough to take her daughter's penchant for death on her shoulders.' And about Lisana's obsession with suicide, he said, 'There is a sense of power in playing with your life.'

Bernie was a sort of sounding board during the years I tried to understand the reasons behind Gladys's comings and goings on the train. I would bring him somewhat haphazardly the new details from my investigation, we would put them in the pile with what we knew already, and while the new concoction was setting and we were having a coffee, I would leave him to his thoughts. After coffee and the long pause that followed, I knew that commentary would emerge that would shed light here and there on my understanding of events. The commentary often wouldn't be meant for me. It had travelled a long path and settled into the depths of his thoughts. I think it was his role as a remote observer that let him be so flexible and free-thinking.

This is not the case for Suzan, who was too close to the events. She is behind the flurry of phone activity that followed on the heels of Gladys from Chapleau until they lost her in the confusion of train lines and pointless suppositions. Suzan has a remarkable memory. Nothing is missing, everything is there; her account of the disarray was flawless. It is almost as if she took notes as her phone buzzed and as her thoughts grew muddled and unmuddled.

So I could have avoided the trip to Chapleau. I already knew from Suzan the little there was to know about Gladys's brief and mysterious trip to Chapleau. But a group of veterans of the school train were expecting me, and I didn't want to miss out on their stories.

In Chapleau I didn't have a single conversation like those I had with Suzan in the little house under the trees. The people I met, all welcoming hosts, were exceedingly generous when it came to telling me about their beautiful, marvellous life on the school train but evasive as soon as a shadow appeared in the conversation. But I spent wonderful evenings with them nonetheless.

Chapleau. It's a strange place. A town of a thousand residents (1,170 according to the last census) that appears to have none, things are so still, with no noise or movement, a sea of tranquility – an inland sea, set in the middle of nowhere, with the closest town a two-hour drive away. There used to be a different sort of life there. You can feel the former busyness under the sleepiness. At least that was the impression I had alighting from the Budd Car. Probably because there were so many tracks leading to the station and so little activity around it.

The Ménards, Ronnie and Marta, were expecting me. They had been warned of my arrival by Suzan. Ronnie is a francophone but speaks such bad French that we quickly switched to English. His wife is a unilingual anglophone. Her parents were Finnish, but she lost her language at the same time as she lost a 't' in her first name (Martta, previously) to become as Canadian as they come. The same thing for Ronnie, who was originally called Ronald.

I stayed with them (they wouldn't hear of me going to a hotel – Chapleau has three!) in their large, ultra-sophisticated house where they raised their five children, who were now scattered to the wind. I say 'ultra-sophisticated' not because of the value or refinement of the furniture or decor, but because the blinds go up and down on their own, the lamps go on as you approach, your bedroom door opens at the sound of your voice, and a dumbwaiter brings you your coffee in the morning as soon as you set foot on the floor; an escalator might as well set you in your chair for breakfast. It is so futuristic that I started to think I would see Yoda or some other creature from another planet appear. Ronnie is a compulsive do-it-yourselfer, a fanatic of technology and gadgets of all sorts, and he dreamed up and perfected everything his knowledge, skills, and crazy ideas permitted him to experiment with in his house, a house they are now prisoners of (it is unsellable – who is going to pay money for a house in Chapleau?), Marta more than him, Marta who confided in me that she would leave 'this armpit' any time (one of the few sounds of discord heard in Chapleau; Marta does not participate in the general enthusiasm).

I spent four days in their high-tech house, and during those four days, I was the king of the carnival. They dragged me to this neighbour's and that neighbour's, all former pupils of the school train, all very old, who welcomed me with coffee, a heap of sandwiches, and cake, their usual meal at the end of the evening, from what I understand.

There was John Keller (age sixty-three, missing three fingers, which he lost in a sawmill), Christopher Young (older, a good musician – how his mother had managed to drag a piano into the forest, I don't know), Varpu Armala (of Finnish origin – her cardamom cake was a delicacy), Matti Valitorppa (also Finnish), and Joe and Rose Gabriel, the only couple of the lot, aside from Ronnie and Marta, my hosts. They enjoyed these get-togethers. Sometimes Christopher played a bit of piano, Joe and Rose danced a little, they laughed, kidded around, told the story of their lives in the woods as if it were a fairy tale. Not one sad, bitter note, no sorrow about how hard life is in the forest, everything was bursting with joy and pride. To hear them you would think there were only happy times along the school train line, except sometimes there was a false note or two from Marta, who would lend a bit of grit to the conversation.

I recorded it all, noted everything (their names, their ages, etc.) on Bernie's recommendation. My iPhone is filled with their old stories. I would put it in the centre of the table, and I would let the conversation roll.

What did I take away from it? Great nostalgia and their refusal to dwell on anything. Even John's missing fingers were material for amusing stories. They had a distinguished guest, *a young man* (I was forty-three at the time) who had made the long journey just to hear what they had to say, and they were not going to hold back. If I would have arrived from Papua New Guinea, I would have had the same effect.

The evenings were pleasant. Their cheer is contagious, and I was filled with stories of the school train. There were moments when I felt like I had a class from the school train around me, they were so *there*, these old children of the forest caught up in their memories.

Rose told the story of her first day on the school train: 'I wasn't even five years old, still too young for school, and I cried my eyes out when I saw my sisters leave in the morning, dressed in their Sunday best with ribbons in their hair. I cried so hard that my mother eventually gave in. One fine morning, I had ribbons in my hair too, and, arriving at the school train, my sisters said to Mr. Campbell, "This is our little sister, Rose," and, as simple as that, I had my first day of school. Mr. Campbell gave me a sheet of paper and crayons. On the sheet, I remember it clearly, there was the outline of a rooster to colour. But I didn't dare. It was too pretty for me to scribble on. I had never coloured anything in my life. Everything was too beautiful around me. My head was spinning from it, I was swivelling in my chair to take in everything. And then, at the end of the afternoon, I fell asleep with my head on the desk. When I woke up, Mrs.

Campbell was there, bent over her sewing machine – I was in their living room! It was so much to take in!'

Matti told the story of an Ojibwe man who arrived one morning with his two children. He stayed with them for school that day, all three sitting cross-legged on desks. At the end of the day, the father thanked Mr. Campbell for having given his children an education, and he took them back into the woods. 'We never saw them again.'

The clickety-clacks came up again in conversation and were no longer a source of amusement. Suzan is 'a little clickety-clack herself,' Marta said. 'Only in Metagama can you soothe yourself counting train cars.'

There was another game, almost as contemplative as Suzan's Clickety-Clacks, that I find sad. You would have to feel you don't belong in the world to have invented it. And, in fact, the game was called At the End of the World. It was their favourite pastime to stand along the tracks when a passenger train went by and wave as the cars passed, hoping a traveller would look out the window, notice one of them, wave back, and the lucky person, the one who was waved at, could fantasize that a stranger was carrying their image to a faraway world. 'It was our way of travelling.' And naturally, everyone thought the stranger was waving at them, and everyone took the trip of their dreams. 'I went to Montreal, Toronto, and Winnipeg.' (That was Christopher, I think.) 'I made trips to Vancouver several times.' (Varpu, a reedy little voice, barely audible.) 'For me it was always Rome.' (Ronnie.) 'Yeah, where else would a Catholic and papist go?' (Christopher.) 'We can't play anymore, what with only the Budd Car left – who wants to go to White River?' (Marta, obviously.)

I listened several times to the bit about At the End of the World, and every time I wondered where my sadness came from. Children hailing dreams when a train went by: there is, undeniably, poetry in that. The image is laden with solitude, though. Children lost in the middle of the forest who have only the track to amuse them and who as old folks still enjoy it like a princely gift: I have a hard time piecing that together.

I listen to the recording again and I hear: 'The railway was our life.' It is Varpu or Christopher or someone else. The words are the end or the start of a story, and I understand that the railway was the lifeline for the forest communities, their only connection to the world. Everything came to them by train. Their provisions, the mail, orders from Eaton's, a visit from a distant relative, good news and bad news, games, dreams, and the marvellous school on wheels. 'We cried with joy when we would see the school train arrive.' (Not all, it seems, because you had to have finished your homework and lessons for the month, and there were dunces among them – Ronnie, for instance.)

They were children of the rails as much as they were children of the forest, and many of them continued to live their lives on the railway. They became brakemen, conductors, telegraph operators, dispatchers. Except for Ronnie, who left school at twelve, barely knowing how to read, write, and count, who became a stationary machinery mechanic in the sawmills in Chapleau and elsewhere, and who was snapped up at top dollar. Which explains the voice-operated doors and the coffee that would arrive by dumbwaiter in the morning.

Ronnie's is a true success story, both for him and for the school train, even though it didn't manage to take him to the end of his schooling. It is a story with two words: *Popular Mechanics*. It all started there, a magazine spotted on the school train bookshelf on young Ronnie's first day of school.

The full-colour cover showed the cross-section of an aircraft cockpit. After that day, the little boy who was both ignorant of and hungry for the world had only one idea in mind: to learn to decode the signs that would let him read what was in the magazine. The rest of the curriculum didn't interest him. When he no longer had trouble getting through *Popular Mechanics*, he quit school to go work at the sawmill in Nemegos, where they took him on as a labourer. But he never failed to show up at the school train for each month's issue. If Ronnie missed it and the school train was already at the next school stop, he would happily walk ten, fifteen, or twenty kilometres, through rain, snow, a blizzard, or temperatures of minus-forty degrees to catch up with the precious bookshelf and his magazine.

More than the career as an expert in industrial mechanics, it is the image of young Ronnie walking all those kilometres along the railway track that I remember from the story. A boy of twelve, thirteen, fourteen, walking through the snow and the shadows of the night (the return trip was made at dusk), fearing nothing because he has the tracks in front of him.

'The tracks were our life.' The words kept coming back, a nostalgic refrain in the weathered music of the aged, and I understood these words, which I also heard time and again: 'Gladys is from the tracks,' and that explains, they believe, her flight along the Northern rails. They needed no other motivation. Gladys was born on the school train, spent many wonderful years there, met her Albert there. Everything that was good and beautiful in life was given to her by the rails. 'It's no surprise that she took the train that morning.' They believe that, on the morning of September 24, Gladys set out on the rails with no itinerary in mind, not thinking about what came next, 'like a bottle in the ocean,' a bottle that would drift along on one train and then another, no matter the direction. What was important was to be carried, tossed, rocked in a steel hull, similar to where she had come into this world.

'And Lisana?

'Lisana …' (There was hesitation, heavy with what went unsaid, and they launched into explanations that explained nothing but their refusal to dwell on a topic that made no sense.)

There was no evening of sandwiches, cake, and coffee with Gladys the last time she visited Chapleau. She arrived on a Thursday afternoon, left the next morning, and essentially didn't leave her bedroom at the Ménards', where I would also sleep (the second time we would sleep in the same bed, the strange sensation of slipping between the blades of time), and where she also received her coffee by dumbwaiter (their coffee is delicious). She only just made it down for meals.

So why make the trip to Chapleau, just to turn around and leave? The question ricocheted around the table, and there was no convincing answer other than that Gladys set off on her adventure just for the clatter of the rails, the familiar smells, the movement that plucked her out of time, 'her love for the trains and her love …' (I almost choked on my sandwich) '… for Chapleau.'

Her love for Chapleau? A broken-down little town where you could die of boredom?

I didn't say anything of the sort, obviously. There was another town in their eyes, it sparkled, it glowed, and then Rose arrived with her cake – exclamations, congratulations, the sound of dishes – and I lost part of the conversation until I heard 'the summer vacation in the marshalling yard.' Chapleau had become an exciting town with its stores, restaurants, movie theatres, all the bustle of a town sprung up in the middle of the forest. 'The Campbell family spent the summer vacation in the marshalling yard.' The words came back, and once again we were plunged into another beautiful, wonderful story about the school train.

Like all small Northern towns that live and die in the wake of a mine or a sawmill, Chapleau had its glory days. And that was where the Campbells spent the few days between school tours for the stores, the movie theatre, the Sunday service, and the many friends who lived there. The school train would rest on a service track in the marshalling yard. They spent their summer vacation there before buying a cottage on the shores of Biscotasi Lake. One can only imagine the discomfort of the steel hull that served as their home, baking in the sun on its bed of burning hot rails. And the worry of the parents (another protest from Marta) who couldn't stop their children from playing on the tracks. That is why, Marta explained, after a few summers in the sweltering heat of the marshalling yard, they opted for a cottage. At the end of June, they would move everything they could to the summer camp (pots and pans, bedding, food, etc.) and did the reverse when they went back to the tracks in September. Equally happy in June and September, they liked spending time together, carefree and luxuriating in all that space, but by the end of August, both parents and children were impatient to leave their summer camp and get back to the activity of the tracks and the cramped quarters of their mobile digs.

It seems that there was nothing about their lives they didn't love. Not even the sweltering heat of summer, not even the extreme cold of the winter, not even the diet that came largely from cans (including roast beef), not even the incessant noise of the trains, nor the sudden moves in the night (objects flying from wall to wall and them tumbling from their beds), there was nothing about their vagabond life that could tarnish the pleasure they got from it.

As for Gladys, she was the friend people fought over. Not just because she was the teacher's daughter, not only because she lived in a dream car (flush toilet, linoleum, etc.), but because she was a dream herself. Likeable, lively, bubbly, always laughing, attentive to everyone … I won't list all of her qualities, because I will grow weary.

The boys were secretly in love with her and were crestfallen when she set her heart on the most feral among them. Ronnie compared them as a couple to Beauty and the Beast. Not that Albert Comeau was repulsive or unkind or depraved in any way. He was a silent boy, withdrawn, attentive in class but not a good student, who at recess was more inclined to follow a hare's tracks than to join in the children's games. 'And not particularly handsome,' Marta added. 'Not really ugly either, but still, you had to wonder what she saw in him.'

A bottomless pit of melancholy was what Gladys found. A well of dark night to lose herself in, she who was so lively and jovial but didn't have enough sun to brighten his days. I had a long conversation with Suzan about it, and she didn't offer any other explanation for Gladys's attraction to a boy so lost in his thoughts. 'She had found someone to give what she had too much of.'

He was the son of a trapper who had his camp near the Nemegosenda River eight kilometres from the tracks. The young Albert made the trip to class by canoe with his little sister. Along the way, they stopped at a point in the river to pick up two young Ojibwe children. In winter, they got to school by dogsled. It was a pretty dangerous mode of travel for schoolchildren who were all of, what? Twelve? Fourteen?

'Albert was ten at the time, his little sister six, and the two Ojibwe boys were about the same age.'

— 76 —

My eyes must have flown open in surprise (and disapproval – what sort of parents let their children travel that way on a river, which by definition is not calm waters?) because Ronnie hurried to explain that in the forest, children grew up fast. And Marta added: 'But it doesn't make for children who are good at school.'

If there weren't parents who could help with lessons and homework during the long month when the school train was teaching children to read and write elsewhere, students left to their own devices got lost in the mishmash of abstract concepts that were as foreign to them as the Empire State Building. This was how it was for children of immigrants and Ojibwe children, whose parents spoke no English, the language of the school train. It was how it was for Albert Comeau, son of a francophone father and an Ojibwe mother.

'He had a hard time concentrating on verb conjugation, so when it came to history, how could you expect the poor boy to understand the Treaty of Westminster?'

And who came to the rescue of the poor boy when he was struggling with a verb or calculating fractions? Gladys, obviously, princess of knowledge and light, who would sit next to him and guide him through the snares of grammar and math. They were prepubescent and then adolescent; no one was on the lookout for feelings developing, not even them, who thought their only tie was schoolwork, except Suzan, with whom Gladys would share confidences in their narrow little bed. Albert had long *slender* hands, Albert had a *purring* voice, Albert had *feline* gestures, Albert's eyes *took you into distant waters*, Albert had something the other boys didn't, he was *different, unique, the only one of his species*, and Suzan understood before anyone else that Albert and Gladys were a couple in the making.

Of the unlikely couple they eventually made, I retain the image Ronnie created. Beauty, because Gladys was indeed a pretty girl (I saw her wedding photo), with a promising future (she had her teaching diploma), everything you could wish for in life, and she went and chose a young man who was not unintelligent but who had no future other than the forest (in the picture, he looks uncomfortable in his suit), the Beast – 'I say that without malice; Albert was a friend.'

Latent during the years on the school train, their love became official when they were seen arm in arm on the streets of Chapleau, 'him with hair as black as a crow, hers blond as wheat,' just happy to be breathing the same air and walking in step.

Gladys was willing to live anywhere with her Albert; she was prepared to follow him into the forest, but Albert didn't want a cabin in the middle of the woods for his princess, and he is the one who walked away from his life. When he found out they were looking for miners in Swastika, he brought his young wife there, and they made their home in the little house on Avenue Conroy. 'The rest is history.'

Gladys and Albert's love story ended on that discreet 'the rest is history.' They weren't going to dwell on the matter. In fact, almost immediately, Rose (or Varpu – I often confuse their voices) hastened to add: 'Chapleau was the town where she fell in love …'

They wanted me to understand that it was out of a sense of romance that Gladys made that impromptu trip to Chapleau. Romance that seemed incongruous from such old people. But I didn't cast doubt on what they were saying, and I wouldn't have succeeded anyway. These men and women are fortresses; their convictions are impenetrable. They can say what they like, but they had a harsh life in the middle of the forest. But not once during our evenings together did I hear them complain about it. Quite the contrary. They are proud of their microwaves, their large-screen TVs, the many gifts life has given them after years of hard work. More than once I had to rave about a glass-top stove or a pleather armchair. And then be rewarded with a smile that radiated the joy of having arrived at their singsong future.

They do not have the souls of complainers, and Gladys will remain in their memories a woman forever in love with a man whose presence she wanted to find again on the trains.

I left Chapleau on the Sunday Budd Car (just one hour late – 'You got lucky,' Ronnie said), steeped in their stories and their optimism. I had the feeling that somewhere there awaited a life that would smile down on me with all of its goodness.

I got lucky, as Ronnie said, with just an hour's wait. That wasn't the case for Gladys, who waited seven hours at the Ménards' before the Budd Car took her to another train, then another, a cavalcade.

Delays on trains in the North aren't a matter of a few minutes or even a few hours. If you don't take the precaution of asking about the predicted delay for your train, you can wind up waiting an entire night at a station at the end of the world, alone or with other equally lonely travellers. The locomotives are from another age, and the track crosses long distances in isolated territory. A rockslide or a mechanical breakdown can stop the already slow advance of the train (never more than fifty miles an hour), not to mention that in summer the intense heat reduces the speed to five miles an hour, and your train that was already a milk run becomes a snail.

All this means that you never know when you're going to board the train or when you're going to get off and, if you're a regular, you don't wait at the station. In Chapleau, for instance, you wait at home or at your hotel after having called the Riverside Motel. That's where the Budd Car crew stays, the ones who take over from the crew that makes the trip from White River, and the receptionist at the Riverside Motel tells you how much longer you have to wait. No one gets impatient, no one grumbles, it's just the way it is.

I am at the fifth day of Gladys's journey, which until now has been simply a little trip to stretch her legs, which anyone could track and comment upon. After Chapleau, or rather, after Metagama, it will be a cavalcade, because at Metagama, in the middle of the night, Suzan will barge into the Budd

Car, and from that point on no one will be able to track what would become a frantic race.

But I'm getting ahead of myself.

Gladys had slept at the Ménards', had had her morning coffee, and well before 1:15 in the afternoon was ready to take the Budd Car, which wouldn't arrive, didn't arrive, until 8:00 p.m. This time the delay was due to the locomotive battery, which for reasons unknown had run down.

A long seven-hour wait coupled with intense phone activity.

Those around Gladys were worried. From Swastika to Metagama to Chapleau, people phoned each other to find out whether she had slept well, whether the cough had worsened, whether she had shown signs of fever. From Swastika to Metagama to Chapleau, people were convinced that she was in no shape to continue the trip.

Suzan was at the centre of the telephone tag. Frank Smarz and Ronnie Ménard didn't know each other, so she was the one to pass information between them. The weather had improved, satellite communication was good, the trains went by her door without her having to pay attention. She waited, took calls, made calls, got tangled up in the calls, trying to understand what was starting to take shape in her mind.

She had phoned Lisana early in the morning. To reassure her ('Your mother is fine, she is in Chapleau at the Ménards"), wish her a nice day ('It's nice and sunny here, is it nice there too?'), and convince her to do what she had to do to get to the end of the day. She knew how hard it was. So she didn't get too worried when she heard Lisana's anguished 'I can't.' 'Come on, it's not that hard. Pull back the curtains, look at the beautiful sun outside. It's the first step that counts. The rest happens all on its own.'

She kept her on the phone for a while. She spoke slowly, carefully, leaving long silences for Lisana, who didn't say anything except, from time to time, 'It's too hard,' which Suzan whittled away at, wore down, buffed to make it 'just a grain of sand, a tiny little grain of sand, trust me, it will pass in no time.' The conversation ended with no resolution from Lisana and the promise from Suzan that she would call her back that night.

All day, Suzan wondered whether she should call her back. She dialled the number a few times, but then put the phone down. She was afraid of Lisana's reaction, that she might feel harassed and stop taking her calls. It was only a little after 8 p.m., when she had confirmation that Gladys was headed toward Sudbury, that she had the conversation that convinced her to light a fire alongside the track to intercept the Budd Car.

But I'm getting ahead of myself again.

It was September 28, the fifth day of the train journey, and Gladys has just boarded the Budd Car. She will meet Janelle, who will be my beacon in what Gladys was thinking. She was her travel companion and, surprisingly, her confidante. I say surprisingly because Janelle is not the kind of person people confide in. She will also be my point of no return. I will never again want to abandon this investigation.

Janelle is a wanderer, there is no other word for it. She comes and she goes, place to place, with such flimsy, tenuous reasons to move from point A to point B that one wonders whether it is all merely to keep her teetering, out of reach, sheltered outside of time. It's no surprise that the two women connected on the Budd Car. At this point in her life, Gladys was also a wanderer.

Janelle was coming from White River, where she had been a waitress at the Mitz Café, and was going to take another job as a waitress almost a thousand kilometres away, in Clova, at the only restaurant going. The reason she left her job in White River was as senseless ('the boss had bad breath') as the one that would take her to Clova (there was an internet beau).

There is something about her that attracts your attention without you quite knowing why. Something off-balance, I would say, both in her movements and her features. At first glance, she is a rather plain woman, late thirties, early forties, nothing remarkable, except that she never stops moving. Abundant hair that she puts up in a complicated arrangement or lets fall in thick, wild clumps. Almost always the same uniform: tight jeans, a thin black camisole under a fleece jacket, and, on her feet, no matter the season, big white running shoes. Nothing particularly noticeable. But it doesn't take long for her to catch your attention. A slight disjointedness in her movements, as if each of her gestures were restrained for a nanosecond. There is also something hesitant in her eyes, a point that moves between her features to create the impression of a shifting space between her longish nose, her mouth, and her eyes, which are a pretty golden brown, very mobile. It's quite unsettling. Her beauty reveals itself up close. At night, when she sleeps, everything falls back into place, nothing moves anymore, and she is the most beautiful woman there is.

Janelle is a seasoned traveller. She knows what you can't expect on the Northern trains, and she boarded the Budd Car with a well-stocked cooler, a blanket, and a pillow for the long trip ahead. At Chapleau, she didn't get off to stock up like the other travellers coming from White River. She had barely dipped into her cooler. Which wasn't the case for the other passengers, who had emptied theirs during the breakdown that had them waiting seven hours for a backup locomotive to arrive from Sudbury. It's a well-known fact that the Budd Car has nothing to offer passengers, not even a glass of water.

So the only people left in the car were her and the old woman, sitting on opposite sides of the aisle.

'She hadn't moved in her seat. It was fascinating, how still she was. A man and a woman just as old had accompanied her to her seat. They said endless goodbyes with a thousand and one recommendations for the trip, her health, the return trip, rest. She smiled, coughed, agreed, coughed some more. It was a terrible cough. But it was clear that all she wanted was for them to go and leave her in peace. After they left, she let out a long sigh, and then I saw her turn into a pillar of salt.'

Janelle doesn't like old people. They scare her. She's always worried they are going to die on her watch. And that is the worst thing that could happen to her, since she runs away from responsibility and is scared to death of death. So they made a strange pair going train to train, night and day, until the old woman couldn't do it anymore.

Gladys was the one who made the first move. Janelle had turned her back to her statue of a neighbour and took advantage of the stop at Chapleau to call friends all over the place (there's no WiFi or cellphone network on Northern trains). She spoke loudly, sometimes in English, sometimes in French, sometimes in both in a single conversation, a single sentence (she is Franco-Ontarian and therefore perfectly bilingual). She was trying, in fact, to reach her sister in Montreal, where she had a room in which she stored her things. That room was the only anchor in her vagabond life.

'Are you going to Montreal?' The question caught her off guard; she had completely forgotten the old woman. Gladys had to repeat the question for Janelle to realize that the woman who was speaking to her was the same one who had been immobile a few moments earlier in the seat across from her. The woman was smiling widely, not as old when she smiled, and she was waiting for an answer to her question.

Janelle answered that she was passing through Montreal, but that she was going farther, much farther, to Clova, a place no one knows, and then, as is done between travellers, she enquired as to the woman's destination. Gladys hesitated a moment (Janelle got the impression she was improvising), then said, 'I'm going to Toronto' (and then another moment of hesitation, the impression of improvisation grew), 'but I may go on to Montreal.'

Janelle believes that is the moment she was chosen, that from her salt-pillar observatory, Gladys had observed her, sized her up, missed nothing of what she said on the phone, and chose her for some unknown reason.

The other travellers returned, the Budd Car started rolling, the two women returned to their thoughts, and the softness of the night gradually enveloped them in its pale blue cotton batting.

Neil McNeil, the conductor, doesn't remember the two travellers, and yet they were the only women on board; there was nothing noteworthy until Metagama.

He had a lot on his mind. He had left two fishing parties along the line three days before, and now he had to pick them up despite the seven-hour delay and the dark night. The first group consisted of three men, regulars. They got off at Biscotasi Lake with their motorboat, fishing gear, jerrycans, and a big plastic barrel that contained their tent and provisions. Neil McNeil had helped them unload their equipment from the freight car. They had agreed on the day and approximate time the Budd Car would pick them up. The same thing for the second group of anglers, who got out north of Wakami Lake. Neil McNeil is used to these chancy rendezvous, which worked out most of the time, but they were problematic this time because of the extremely long delay. He kept leaving his passengers to go to the train driver's cab to make sure there was enough visibility on the track.

'The train station at Clova is pretty ...'

The old woman was trying a new approach. Janelle had again forgotten her. Nice and warm under her blanket (the night had grown cooler), she was listening to Shania Twain on her iPhone. Gladys repeated what she had said about the Clova train station, and Janette took out her earbud.

'She had eyes like embers, but blue like the sea, eyes that burned, feverish eyes that looked deep into mine, and she was shivering.'

'It was the only thing to do: I offered her my blanket. The woman was sick. You know me, I'm no Mother Teresa. I'm not the type to go around saving humanity, but it was the only thing to do.'

So Janelle crossed the aisle to cover Gladys with her blanket and sat down beside her just to talk about the place, Clova, where she had never been but that Gladys knew well. She was about to go back to her seat when Gladys did something surprising: she spread part of the blanket over Janelle. (We wondered long and hard, Janelle and I, over what to think; did Gladys at that point feel so weak that she needed a travel companion? Or did she already have in mind what she was going to entrust her with?) It was a decisive move. From that point on, the two women didn't leave each other's side.

Janelle felt trapped but didn't resist, because it looked like it would be an interesting conversation. Gladys had a lot of stories to tell. She had travelled almost all of Canada by train, trips that had their share of adventure, and obviously she told her about the school train in great detail, as was her habit. Janelle also had stories to tell, not all happy ones, that took place on the rails or the road, which she contributed to the conversation with a deadpan tone, as if none of her stories concerned her, only to give Gladys a rest. Janelle doesn't have much interest in herself or her life, however adventurous it is, so I got only pieces of it here and there. Before the trains, there was the road. Janelle had had several cars, minivans mostly, into which she would cram her essential possessions and that became her mobile home. She would go from place to place, taking a job as a waitress, a cook, a cleaner; whatever it was, the important thing was that the job keep her afloat for a while, at least until the boss did or said something she didn't like, until the lover of the day made some mistake, any excuse to hit the road again for another motel, hotel, or restaurant, preferably somewhere at the end of an isolated road where she would disembark as an alien. And she was now on the trains because she had lost her driver's licence for reasons she refused to tell me (drinking and driving, I'm pretty sure – she loves to be drunk as much as she loves to be free).

The two women kept talking, curled up under their blanket, while the Budd Car sliced through the night at an unusual speed to make up for the delay.

The first stop, to bring the people who had been fishing at Wakami Lake on board, brought a gust of cold air into the car. The party, a man in his fifties and a young couple, were visibly relieved to be on board, but, without making a big thing about the long hours spent waiting near the railway track, they started down the aisle, trailing in their wake the cold night. The man greeted Neil McNeil with a clap on the shoulder, 'Good to see you, my friend,' and they calmly took their seats.

The arrival of the fishing party created a bit of a stir in the general sleepiness. People started talking again in low voices. The car was bathed in a bluish light. The hum of voices accompanied the rattling of the car. It made for a hoarse, gentle music, a lullaby modulated to the swaying of the car sometimes broken up by Gladys's deep, wheezing cough and, soon, in the steel hull wrapped in the night, all that remained were the murmuring voices of the two women and soon, nothing: Gladys had dozed off.

Janelle wanted to take the opportunity to return to her seat, but she had barely twitched when she felt Gladys's hand slide onto her thigh and squeeze it.

'I sat there wondering what I was going to do with this old woman. There was no doubt about it. She had glommed on to me. I couldn't get rid of her. She was old and sick, and she had decided that she would travel with me or I would travel with her. I don't know who was travelling with who in her mind.'

What worried her was the transfer for Toronto. It was already complicated enough, and if, on top of it, she had to trail a sick old woman behind her, it was going to be even trickier. Janelle had made the trip from White River to Montreal many times, and she knew that the worst part was catching the connection to Toronto. The Budd Car would drop her at the station in downtown Sudbury however much behind schedule, and she had to immediately jump in a taxi to get to the other station ten kilometres north of the city, in no man's land, an industrial area where not a soul lived. The station opened only at midnight in anticipation of the arrival of the train, scheduled for 1:15, but that could keep you waiting until dawn. Janelle remembered the feeling of being god knows where waiting for a ghost train in a ghost station.

Behind the black screen of the window, she couldn't see the villages stream by in the night. From the hammering of the wheels against the joints of the track (the clickety-clacks so dear to Suzan's and Gladys's hearts), she knew that the Budd Car was moving at maximum speed and that they might arrive in time to catch the Sudbury–Toronto train, if it was delayed enough. Otherwise she would have to find a hotel room for her and the old woman, because she had resigned herself to not abandoning her.

The stop at Biscotasi Lake seemed to her to take forever. They had to hoist into the freight car all the fishing equipment (boat, etc.), which slid from their hands in the dark, and it was only after fifteen long minutes that Janelle saw in the aisle behind Neil McNeil the three smiling fishermen joking about the local bears they had time to make friends with, their only comment about the wait in the cold night before dropping into their seats and falling asleep almost immediately.

With no other stops on its itinerary, the Budd Car got back up to speed, to Janelle's great relief.

Twenty minutes later, there was the screech of wheels on the track as the Budd Car's emergency brakes were applied:

fire was blazing near the track at Metagama. Someone was signalling they wanted to come aboard. Suzan.

Suzan in slippers and pyjamas, with just a wool jacket thrown over her, an angry Suzan.

She had phoned Lisana a few hours earlier, and she was seething with helplessness and indignation. Helplessness because all she had was her instinct and a few words from Lisana to convince her of the urgency of the situation. And indignation against herself. She had been pathetic, she had failed pathetically. She hadn't found the right words to say to Lisana, and worse, she had said the thing she shouldn't have. Suzan would have liked to start the conversation over, to listen to Lisana, really listen to her, her voice, her tone of voice, its exasperated slowness, when she said, 'I can't do it anymore.' She should have grasped the nuance. Lisana was beyond her *I can't do it*, she was at the end of her rope. She couldn't do it *anymore*. And Suzan, rather than paying attention to the weight of the words, gave her the usual spiel. 'Yes, you can do it. You're stronger than you think. Believe me, you can do it.' Then Lisana, even more exasperated: 'No, I've tried and I've tried. I can't do it anymore.' Suzan didn't know how to keep on encouraging her, telling her over and over, 'It's the first step that's the hardest, the rest just takes care of itself,' while at the other end of the line she heard, 'I can't do it anymore,' repeated with increasing desperation and finally, in a flat voice, 'My hand just won't, my hand can't do it anymore,' to end the conversation. Lisana had hung up.

Lisana was in crisis. There was no doubt about it. Suzan called back immediately, no answer. She called and called again, still no answer. No answer at the Smarzes' either. It was almost midnight, and she remembered that the Smarzes were in the habit of disconnecting the phone before going to bed.

Lisana was in crisis, and Gladys was off gallivanting on the train. There was nothing to understand, except that she had to do something, and fast. But what?

Suzan built the fire and didn't have to wait long before the light of the Budd Car appeared in the night.

When he saw her climb into the car in pyjamas (he didn't have time to lower the steps), Neil McNeil thought her son had had an emergency, but he soon understood that this wasn't about her son.

What followed was reported to me in great detail by Janelle, Suzan, and Neil McNeil, although none of them had the same understanding of what happened.

Momentary madness, is what Neil McNeil thought. The momentary madness of a hermit. Living in a cabin in the middle of the woods with only your thoughts as company, sometimes old anger, old pain, can bubble up to the surface, and everything gets confused. You have to be strong to resist it. I have seen a raving lunatic board the train screaming his head off that he was going to kill someone, who and why I never knew, maybe he didn't know himself. He was old, over eighty. There are no young forest hermits. You have to have a life behind you to have something to think about when you go deep into the woods. That one should have been long dead in his cabin, but he had the time to get to the train before having his brain addled by someone who did something shitty to him from another life. Like Suzan when she arrived in her pyjamas and ran down the aisle like a chicken with her head cut off. Suzan is not a true hermit. She has a phone, the train that goes by her house, and her son Desmond who comes to see her every week. And she's not old enough to have her brain addled. But there was a short-circuit, a compulsion, that was sure. She wouldn't stop shouting: "Get back home now. She's going to do it.'"

When she told me the whole story in the little house under the trees, Suzan had a hard time explaining how she had become a hysterical old woman screaming like a lunatic in the Budd Car. In the moment, she said, she wasn't even aware she was screaming. Her brain just kept playing in a loop, a blade sunk into Lisana's wrist, and that image didn't jibe, 'I mean, not at all,' with Gladys's calm assurance. 'She was speaking to me as if I were a child who had just had a nightmare.'

'Easy, Suzan, calm down. Nothing is going to happen.'

'Calm down? Lisana is going to do it. You should have heard her. I just spoke to her on the phone.'

'There's no need to worry, Suzan. She's not going to do it.'

'I'm telling you she is. She's going to do it.'

'I'm telling you she isn't. She's not capable of it anymore.'

'She's going to do it. I'm telling you. Get back to Swastika now.'

'Believe me, she hasn't been capable of it for some time now.'

'Go home, Gladys. I'm begging you. She's going to do it, I swear.'

'You don't need to worry. Nothing is going to happen.'

Despite her reassuring words, Gladys wasn't calm or peaceful under the blanket she was sharing with Janelle. 'She was extremely tense, frozen stiff, a steel bar, her fingers digging into my thigh.'

Around them a confused murmur of sleepy voices protested weakly. Neil McNeil approached, tried to calm Suzan down, but it was like trying to drive back a furious sea. Suzan was shouting louder and louder. There was a minefield between the two women, the cutting edge of a sharp ridge. The exchange grew narrower, closed off. Janelle felt it in the hand on her thigh that became like an eagle's grip ('I had bruises'). There was no way out. An increasingly hysterical Suzan was ordering Gladys to go home to Swastika immediately, and Gladys, in the same calm voice, the same firm hand under the blanket, kept repeating that she was worrying for nothing.

The sleepers, now fully awake, were complaining loudly. Neil McNeil, well aware of the growing delay, was trying to calm both Suzan and his passengers at the same time. Then, seeing one of them get up looking like he meant trouble, he said, 'Make up your mind, Suzan. Are you staying on or getting off? Decide now, because we have time to make up.' And to make the urgency of the situation crystal clear, he added, indicating Janette: 'She has to catch the Sudbury–Toronto train.'

And this is where the knot of confusion is created; this is where Gladys's trail was lost for good, because Suzan never would have left the Budd Car – 'I would have stayed, even in slippers and pyjamas. I would have stayed in the Budd Car. I would have gone with her to Swastika' – if Gladys hadn't told her what she wanted to hear.

'Don't worry, Suzan. I'll go back to Swastika. I'll get the Northlander in Toronto with my young friend. We'll be in Swastika by the afternoon.'

Pure fabrication, the *young friend* thought as she felt the hand relax its grip and pat her on the thigh. Gladys was asking her not to contradict her.

Janelle was now certain that the woman was on the run. She was fleeing something, someone, her own home; regardless of what she was running from, there was this screaming hyena who wanted to bring her back to her point of departure. And Janelle, completely loyal, because she herself was always on the run, said nothing.

There was a menacing commotion around Suzan. A passenger had stood up, a large man, six feet tall, all muscles and rage. He headed toward Suzan. She had no choice; she had to take Gladys at her word and leave the car of her own volition. She knows now that that is when Gladys slipped into the quicksand of questions without answers. She slipped away.

After Suzan left, calm was restored, and the Budd Car resumed its journey. There were still another two hours before its destination. The connection for the Sudbury–Toronto train was in serious jeopardy. Janelle knew it but didn't worry about it. She was accompanying an old woman on the run, and she liked the idea.

'Who is Lisana?'

The question wasn't an attempt to untangle the old woman's story. Janelle just wanted to know whether she would be lost in mystery the whole time or whether she would have a signpost or two to guide her through their acquaintance.

'She is my daughter, and she has death in her soul.'

The response came with no hesitation, no emotion.

'She didn't blink, didn't stir – the only thing that was moving was her hand up and down my thigh, a sort of caress, to soothe herself or me, I don't know which.'

'I laid my hand on hers, and we fell asleep against each other. We were still asleep when the train pulled into the station.'

In Sudbury, they took a taxi to the ghost station. The night was cold and inhospitable, the streets filled with partiers, the taxi dirty and smelly, so crossing the city was difficult. The driver kept rolling down the window and shouting at throngs of partiers who were slowing him down and, in some places, stopping him altogether. Janelle was cursing in the back seat. They didn't have much time.

Finally, at the end of a dirt road that crossed an uninhabited area, the little light of the station appeared. That light in the night was a beacon of hope. The station, which opened at midnight, closed as soon as the train went by. Unless, Janelle started to worry, the train had already passed, and the station employee was just hanging around.

He was there, the sole employee on the night shift, in what was possibly a station (from the outside, it looked more like a shed), but he couldn't issue Gladys a ticket, neither electronic, nor paper. Janelle was telling the employee off, using every possible tone to get special authorization, when rumbling announced the train's arrival. The Sudbury–Toronto train was pulling into the *station* (I hesitate to use the word after what Janelle told me about it).

It was two in the morning. Gladys was exhausted, coughing more and more. Janelle, determined to see this adventure through, sat Gladys in a wheelchair that was hanging around (you heard right: a wheelchair in that *station*), headed toward the man in the peaked cap who was coming down the train's footboard, and set about convincing him that they could not abandon a sad-fragile-poor-old woman in such inhospitable surroundings.

The Sudbury–Toronto train isn't a slow Northern milk run. It's the train that leaves from Vancouver, crosses the Rockies and the Prairies, arriving in Toronto four days later. A real train with a dining car, a panoramic dome car (with a spectacular view of the Rockies), sleeping compartments, travellers who come from all over to experience Canada's wide-open spaces, and staff in peaked caps wearing the colours of their employer.

Janelle wasn't dealing with a Neil McNeil or a Sydney Adams. The man she was trying to soften up was not in command of his train. He was a ticket controller in charge of enforcing the company's rules, and, like the station employee, he was not authorized to hand out a passenger ticket. Travellers who take the Sudbury–Toronto train must have one already. Janelle had hers well before her departure from White River.

The only travellers that night at the ghost station were Janelle and the poor woman in the wheelchair. That was their stroke of luck. Because the controller, more embarrassed than sympathetic to the situation, glanced around to make sure there were no witnesses aside from the employee who was bringing up the rear with Janelle's bags. The two men exchanged a look, and Janelle understood that they had reached an understanding that they would break the rule.

That was how they were able to board the Sudbury–Toronto train and continue their journey.

As if she knew she would be the sole repository for a night she would have to tell me about, Janelle committed to memory the conversation they had on the train with the reliability of a tape recorder.

Lisana, it was all about Lisana.

During the long night when the confidences poured out, Gladys described Lisana as a little girl, the light of her life, her joy, her devotion; the teenager who had boys mooning after her and who confided her fears, her dreams, her romantic conquests and disappointments; the nursing student in her first pool of blood, her eyes as hard as stone, who told her in a voice just as hard, *Leave me*; and the other Lisana, the one she became by calling death to herself so many times. It was that last Lisana who came up the most often in her rambling thoughts.

There were long pauses, because speaking wore her out. Around them, everyone was sleeping, people who had made the trip from Winnipeg, Saskatoon, and Vancouver, who were unable to afford a berth, and who slept however they could. The car was silent and comfortable, no swaying, no screeching metal; all that could be heard was the snoring of the sleepers and Gladys's voice in the night, carried on a cushion of air.

Janelle was offering her a level of attention 'I never would have thought myself capable of.' She plumped the pillow, pulled up the blanket that had slid down, swaddled Gladys, made sure the old woman was as comfortable as she could be, and waited for the voice to trail off into a long silence or, even better, into deep sleep, but sleep was 'short, it never lasted long.'

The voice perked up when it emerged from these pauses, but the brain didn't follow. There were memories entwined with what remained of her dreams. There was Albert complaining about a migraine or a hammer he couldn't find, Albert whom she called *my sweet darling*. There was her father or her mother or someone else on the school train who had just announced that the track had wound around a gigantic animal with a long neck that was swallowing clouds. There was one of her mother's recipes that she recited, intoned. But as soon as she snapped out of it, it was all about Lisana again.

Gladys didn't try to give her daughter uncommon, gentle qualities revealed only to intimates – quite the contrary. She told stories of the seedy areas of Toronto she had dragged Lisana out of; she unceremoniously described her as she would find her then, her raving, her evil eye, the madness she hurled at her mother's face, and, when her daughter moved home, the evil eye that came back and brought with it bad times. 'Death was stalking my daughter, or she was summoning death, I never knew, but you have to be able to recognize the evil eye. Don't worry, she doesn't do it anymore. She's not capable of it anymore.' The *don't worry* would repeat through the night.

Janelle doesn't understand how she managed to stay there, why she didn't get up, take a seat at the other end of the car so as not to hear what she didn't want to hear. Death, I think I have said, isn't a subject she is fond of. Death is left to the dead, death doesn't exist unless you talk about it, and she let herself listen for hours to death that was awaited, hoped for, desired, and ultimately didn't come, because Lisana was *no longer capable of it*. But you have to act as though it will come, Gladys said.

The brief periods when Gladys dozed off were the only moments when Janelle could set the darkness to one side. She would let her eyes wander around her and try to distract her thoughts by seizing on some traveller who was snoring not far from her. A young man caught her eye. He was sleeping peacefully, stretched over the two neighbouring seats, never waking up or moving to find a more comfortable position, as if he were in his own bed. The young man – no older than twenty, she thought – offered a pleasant diversion from her thoughts. But already Gladys was emerging from her slumber and in the scattered pieces of her mind came back to her daughter and the evil eye. When a bad turn was on the horizon, Gladys explained, she couldn't handle any noise. They had to turn off the radio, turn off the television, and talk, talk, talk. These were exhausting days, she told Janelle in a single breath, herself exhausted from talking so much, but still continued as if the night were going to close in around her before she had said everything she had to say.

Janelle tried to concentrate on the young man. His socks were what first intrigued her. Two big sturdy feet resting on the arm of the seat, revealing along the sides of the socks long grimy trails that suggested he had been travelling for days without being able to change. From Vancouver? from Winnipeg? she wondered.

The young man's socks were no match for Gladys who, between rambling and dozing, insisted on telling her about all of her daughter's suicidal episodes.

There is a dark joy that shines in her eyes, Gladys said, and agitation that terrorizes and delights her at the same time. You have to get her moving, walk her room to room, anything. You have to take care of her body so that the idea that is holding her captive lets go of her. It's only once you see her eyes empty that you can breathe a little. And then you have to turn everything back on, the television, the radio, everything, full blast. There needs to be a lot of noise, otherwise it starts over again. They are exhausting days, Gladys repeated, but don't worry, she won't do it, she won't do it again, she's not capable of it anymore, but you have to pretend you believe she will.

Day was breaking. They would arrive in Toronto in a few hours. A singsong voice announced the last call for breakfast in the dining car. Janelle took out what remained in her cooler: juice, yogourt, and fruit cups. Gladys refused, Janelle insisted, and Gladys half-heartedly accepted yogourt and juice. Seeing her swallow a handful of pills with her juice, Janelle knew that her travelling companion was a very sick woman.

The young man woke up and was having breakfast, a can of tuna he pulled out of his backpack. An organized traveller who knew how to plan ahead, Janelle thought, as she watched him out of the corner of her eye. A musician, she thought, the shape of a large black case against the oversized backpack leaving no doubt. A guitar – unlikely a violin, what with the AC/DC T-shirt. She was glad he was there.

The car was now filled with sunlight, day had broken, and the approach to Toronto had started, with its industrial parks and condo towers streaming by. Travellers were getting their bags. They were about to arrive at the station when Gladys asked, suggested, proposed (Janelle wasn't sure which word to use): 'If we arrive in time, we could take the Northlander to Swastika.'

The Northlander wasn't waiting for them when they arrived at the station in Toronto. The Northlander had made its last trip the night before. The Toronto–Cochrane passenger line was no more. The announcement of the disappearance of the Northlander had created an uproar in Northern Ontario. But there was too much nostalgia and not enough actual riders among the protesters to stop the march of time, and the Ontario Northland Railway stuck to its decision.

Gladys knew the train schedule as well as she knew her times tables. The protests had started long before her departure from Swastika. So she knew the Northlander wouldn't be there.

The only thing that would explain her strange request of Janelle was her confused state. She had forgotten the day and the time; time was already slipping away from her.

I was on that train. I was on the last Northlander, and it makes my head spin to think that, while I was in the midst of the noisy convoy that was there to greet the last Northlander, not far from me there were people who have become so dear to me and who were struggling with setbacks I am now labouring to write about.

We have an endangered train in Senneterre too, and I was there as president of sos Transcontinental. I had boarded the last Northlander with the feeling that one day I would be making a similar trip in what remained of the Transcontinental. Northern trains are disappearing, and I don't think our little association will manage to save the last section of the Transcontinental. I was there in solidarity with the people of Northern Ontario.

There was a sort of raw celebration on that train. Many people came, members of parliament, mayors, former railway workers, former conductors, former passengers, journalists, and even a train buff (a German man, whom I spotted right away, and with whom I exchanged a few words), all wanting to witness a historic moment. Many of them hadn't seen each other in a long time. There were reunions, rage, impotence, nostalgia, and the desire to be able to say, 'I was there.' I wondered whether we would celebrate the end of our rail era the same way.

It makes my head spin a little to look back, to think I was there on that train, and that the next day Gladys and Janelle pulled into the station in Toronto, too late for the Northlander, and that I went back to my life without knowing that it would take another turn.

I have always had competing desires to both be and not be somewhere else, so this suits me. In this moment, I am an abstraction. I am the observer of a story that will pull me in its wake, and I tell myself that a single day was all that stood between me and being there, near her, in the boisterous celebration that greeted the last Northlander. Who knows what we would have become? Janelle would have appeared long before I actually met her, and I would have been at her side, in the seams of time. Yes, I would have been at her side. This woman was not to be mine; I would have known it as soon as I laid eyes on her, and I would have wanted, painfully wanted, her to feel my eyes upon her, and our story would have started there, on the Northlander, in a crack in time. I have only ever loved women whose inner worlds were not mine and never would be.

If she had been there, on the last Northlander, the little I had with Janelle would probably already be over, and I wouldn't be here wanting to write a story that no longer concerns me.

They were in the main concourse at Union Station, a bit dizzy from the comings and goings of the travellers and the noise that echoed in the massive dome. Janelle had picked up her luggage (I have not yet mentioned her luggage; it was incredible how much she could carry), and they were having a sandwich while watching the stream of travellers go by. Gladys was nibbling on hers. She had only managed to get through a third of it while Janelle had wolfed hers down completely and immediately got on her iPhone. She was trying to reach her sister in Montreal.

No decision had been made. They knew the Northlander was no more, and they were there, lost in that crowd, waiting to see what lay ahead.

Indecision is not typical of Janelle, any more than the contemplation of unfathomable questions is. She is wary of getting existentially bogged down. I often saw how she worked and was astonished each time to see how she found a shortcut when questions took a corner. I have a hard time imagining her sitting in the main concourse at Union Station, or anywhere else, waiting for a decision that wasn't coming.

She had never intended to take the Northlander 'to keep death company, no thank you.' Even before arriving in Toronto, she already had a plan. She was going to put Gladys on the train, *'Enough is enough,'* she would send the mother back to her daughter, and then she would be alone and free, as she had always been, and would continue her journey to her job as a waitress and her internet beau.

But there was no more Northlander, and Gladys was there, by her side, calm in the midst of the bustle of travel, with no destination and seemingly not worried about it.

Janelle would learn that the woman has her own magnetic pole, and, come what may, they would both go where she decided.

Gladys had something in mind, because as soon as Janelle had finished her calls to Montreal (she had finally reached her sister), Gladys asked her to dial her number in Swastika.

'She had a big smile, the same smile as in Chapleau when she approached me.'

She dialled the number and passed her the phone.

'You can't escape Gladys's smile.'

Janelle obviously didn't hear any of what Lisana said to her mother, but it must have been plaintive, judging from Gladys's tone. And repetitive because Gladys kept saying over and over, 'It's okay … it's okay … you don't have to … take your time … Lisana … no one is forcing you … take all the time you need … Lisana … just leave it for today … wait … Lisana … wait …' Then, turning to Janelle with a smile that wouldn't quit despite how obviously heavy the conversation was, Gladys said to her daughter: 'I have someone with me, a friend. Her name is Janelle, and she is going to take the bus to Swastika with me.'

And with no regard for Janelle, who was waving her arms in the air to indicate that there was no way she would be taking that bus ('I was stunned! How could she?'), Gladys handed her the phone, repeating to her daughter that Janelle was a friend, that she would take the bus to Swastika, and that she would love her like a sister.

The voice on the line was not what she expected. She had imagined something gritty, gravelly, 'absolutely not the sweetness of a little girl.' The voice grew fuller as Janelle carefully explained to her that she would not be taking the bus and, with even more tact – because she thought Lisana didn't know – that her mother was sick. 'I know,' said the voice without faltering.

What Lisana said next got lost in a steady stream that Janelle couldn't follow or report coherently, it was so messed up and, she believed, out of touch with reality. There was an obsession with karma, the forces of the universe, light from the phone, neighbours jostling at her door, the neighbours who were against her karma and who were pushing her toward forces that were hostile to her. 'Everyone has their own karma,' Lisana said a number of times, 'and my mother's karma ...' 'And your mother's karma is to take the bus to Swastika,' Janelle interrupted her, unable to take any more of the gibberish.

Now it was Gladys's turn to wave her arms in the air. She would not be taking the bus to Swastika. And it was in that moment, when nothing further was possible, when all ways out were closed, that Janelle felt Gladys's will weave its way to where she didn't expect it. 'Tell her we're taking the train to Montreal,' Gladys whispered in her ear. And Janelle, to her own surprise, heard herself announcing to Lisana: 'Your mother and I are taking the next train to Montreal.' (She heard Lisana's silence on the line as she was thinking.) 'My sister Marie-Luce is in Montreal. She's a nurse, and she will take of your mother's karma.'

'And what then?' Lisana demanded. ('I was furious: this woman wasn't completely insane, she wanted to know my plan!')

Janelle didn't know what then.

But at her side, Gladys's insistent smile grew tense.

'Then you wait for me to phone you.'

Gladys broke into a wide smile. Janelle had said what she was supposed to. ('I felt as though I slipped from my body. I had just obeyed a wish that wasn't my own.')

It was the decision made at Union Station that resulted in Gladys being called a monster. In Toronto, everything was still possible. She could take the bus home to her daughter in Swastika and let Janelle carry on with her trip. Rather than doing that, she abandoned her daughter to her suicidal compulsions to traipse around on trains with a stranger. It was outrageous, vile, absolutely shameful in a mother.

While many judged and criticized, Janelle refused to be outraged. It was in Toronto that she understood that Gladys was not on the run.

'She had a goal, she was after something, and I was her companion without knowing what to expect. She was at the helm, and I was rowing. It wasn't like me to let myself be carried off somewhere in a boat without knowing where I was going. I hardly recognized myself.'

In Toronto, no need to wait for a ghost train for hours; there are nine daily departures for Montreal. They took the 3:15 p.m. train, which would get them to Montreal in the evening.

In Swastika and in Metagama, everyone was in the dark; they had no idea what had become of Gladys and her *young friend* since the Budd Car. Frank Smarz was manning the phone, calling pretty much everywhere, trying to find out whether they had taken the Sudbury–Toronto train, whether from Toronto – and it was what they desperately hoped – they had taken the bus to Swastika, whether this, whether that, a haze of suppositions because they could find no trace of an old woman on the Sudbury–Toronto train, because the ticket controller would not admit that he had allowed a passenger to board without a ticket.

They didn't know what was going on with Lisana either. She had barricaded herself in the house, door closed, curtains drawn, phone off the hook; she would no longer answer the door or Frank Smarz. That was what he explained in an exasperated voice. 'That woman is a curse for everyone.'

Suzan had called Frank Smarz at first light. He was the one who told her the Northlander was no longer running. She had a moment of panic when she realized Gladys would not be going back to Swastika. But she quickly pulled herself together: 'In that case, you'd better go over to Gladys's and stay with Lisana. Don't leave her on her own, otherwise she's going to do it. I'm telling you she's going to do it.' And Frank Smarz said nothing, not a word, a glum silence.

This conversation and the others that followed – because there were many during the course of the day – convinced her that Frank Smarz would not rush to Lisana's rescue.

Suzan fears the dark instinct she has always had in her that allows her to glimpse what is hidden under intentions that won't rise to the surface. As the calls mounted, she slowly realized that no one in Swastika would run to Lisana's side. Deliberately, united, in tacit agreement.

Suzan has known Frank Smarz for years; she knows he is clumsy with his words, unable to express nuanced feelings, and, during that day when everything was in a flurry around him, he was uncharacteristically prudent, weighing and reweighing his words, and repeating with a rare and bewildering patience that she needn't worry about Lisana. The woman had travelled the long road of despair without ever doing what can't be undone, he said. They should be worrying about Gladys instead; they had to figure out how to get her back to Swastika.

The long road of despair, strange words indeed from this man's mouth. His voice, his words, his prudence, his refusal to force open the door or a window ('Good lord, Frank. I'm not asking you to go at it with an axe. A screwdriver, a crowbar, and you're in. It's simple.'), his increasingly expeditious way of cutting short the conversation each time she called, and Suzan's dark instinct went into overdrive.

She came to believe that the neighbourhood friends had abandoned Lisana to her suicidal obsessions so that, when Gladys returned ('and that was all Frank cared about, Gladys's return – nothing else mattered to him'), she would be free of her unhappy daughter.

'I don't trust what I can dream up sometimes. I have often had to take a step back because I scare myself so badly with what my brain can come up with, and in that instance, I was imagining the worst.'

And yet she believed in the dark horrors of her brain. Enough to convince her to make the trip to Swastika. Which was a three-day affair, because she had to wait for her son, who was arriving in the afternoon by Budd Car, wait for the Budd Car the next day to go to Sudbury, and make the trip the day after that with her son and his old clunker of a car to Swastika, not knowing whether she would get there in time.

I spent a long time wondering about the intentions of the neighbourhood friends, and I still don't know what to think. Can friendship lead to passive murder? Can you be guilty of assisted suicide through a failure to assist? Did these people, who welcomed me at their table, who were so generous and likeable when I was travelling regularly to Swastika, were they capable of hiding in their houses, with their good intentions and ill will, waiting for the neighbour to slit her wrists? Gladys's friends and neighbours, ugly, wicked people? Murderers without knowing it?

My friend Bernie was as perplexed as I was. He has known these people forever. He runs into them at the grocery store, the hardware store, soccer games. They are as familiar to him as the air he breathes, as organically connected, and he won't have his air contaminated. But he didn't weigh in, didn't say a word when I told him what Suzan had imagined. It was only later, when we were talking about something completely different, that his concern came back: 'Those are just presumptions, interpretations, nothing concrete – you're going to stick to the facts, right?'

I dread the moment he reads these lines.

Because the presumptions remain. Despite the time that has passed, despite her refusal at times to believe it herself,

Suzan still talks to me with resentment about her arrival in Swastika. The curtains were drawn; nothing was stirring around the house or at the neighbours. No one came to the window to see what was going on. No one came to protect Gladys's house when she arrived with her son and his crowbar ready to pop the hinges of the front door.

I tried different approaches with Frank Smarz, Brenda, and the other neighbourhood friends. I was hoping to clarify this episode, but it is the nature of the unspeakable not to be spoken. I got nothing that would chase away the doubt that Suzan planted in my mind. The neighbourhood friends are doomed to appear in this chronicle with unspecified ill intentions.

Bernie, my friend, if you're there, I ask that you not stop at these lines.

Because the adventure isn't over. There is still a great deal to record and illuminate. Gladys's disappearance on the Northern trains is full of minefields. I am on day six of Gladys's journey, and at this point in the story, there have only been tenuous answers to questions that raise yet others.

On this sixth day, Janelle and Gladys took their seats on the Toronto–Montreal train. They had a five-hour trip ahead of them. They were exhausted. Janelle hadn't really slept since her departure from White River. She settled Gladys in the window seat with a pillow and a blanket and lowered the blind, hoping the cozy nest would do its job and she would be able to sleep too.

A man went down the aisle with the snack trolley. Janelle had a coffee, and Gladys had an orange juice that she swallowed with a handful of pills. A slew of questions from Janelle, no explanation from Gladys.

Gladys was going to drift off. Janelle observed with relief her head sink into the softness of the pillow, eyelids drooping, but before her body completely let go, Gladys had a jolt of energy and asked her in a voice that did not falter, almost with authority: 'You'll call her? Promise me you'll call her.'

Janelle promised, and Gladys let herself fall into a deep sleep. She didn't move an eyelash for the remaining hours.

The car was calm and hushed. Janelle was listening for Gladys's snoring and trying to convince herself to make the call. The people around her were busy on their computers, tablets, and cellphones, people who regularly shuttled between Toronto and Montreal, an anonymous environment that she knew from having often made the trip from White

River to Montreal and that was a break from the friendliness of Northern trains, where you have to respond to all looks, smiles, and invitations, however unwelcome.

Janelle wondered what to say to this woman in a delirium who was probably expecting soothing words, encouraging words, or maybe not; maybe she expected nothing, maybe she just wanted someone at the other end of the line who would agree to follow her in her fantasies, and none of these options did anything to convince her to make the call. She preferred to think about Marie-Luce, her sister, who would be at the station in Montreal. Marie-Luce would know what to do. She always did. She thought of Marie-Luce's apartment. It was nothing fancy, but Janelle had always felt at home there. Gladys could take some time to rest in the bedroom that had been Janelle's for years. They would have to clear it out a bit. It was a mess – Gladys couldn't sleep in the clutter of boxes and garbage bags. As for Janelle, she would sleep with Marie-Luce. For the rest of it, what should be done about Gladys, she would decide with Marie-Luce. And beyond that, the waitressing job and the internet beau waiting for her in Clova, she didn't want to think about that; they would wait. And softly, in the tangle of her thoughts and Gladys's snoring, the exhaustion of the travel overtook her.

She awoke in the commotion that happens right before pulling into the station. A man with a paunch was leaning his weight on her as he tried to extricate his suitcase from the overhead baggage compartment.

Gladys was still sleeping deeply. Janelle hesitated before waking her. She looked younger, her features smoother, her face rounder, almost like a child, completely given over to another world. She allowed her a moment of grace before lightly shaking her. Gladys opened haunted eyes. Her features sagged, the roundness disappeared; everything that had been at rest awoke brutally at the same time as the cough, wet and deep, that wouldn't subside. Between loud wheezing and rattles, she managed to ask: 'Did you call her?' Janelle lied.

'I lied because it was the only thing to do. Her eyes were burning with fever. I told her what she wanted to hear.'

Her sister was there in Montreal, and they took charge of Gladys together, the wheelchair, picking up luggage, heading to the parking lot, and settling Gladys in the front seat. They stuffed the many large bags in the back. Janelle was waiting for the usual reprimands about everything she travelled with. Instead, Marie-Luce, direct and solid Marie-Luce, said to her: 'What have you brought me? That woman is dying.'

I know Marie-Luce, her apartment, her neighbourhood, and her incredible life force. I have stayed at her apartment many times, alone or with Janelle (readers – should I allow them to exist one day – will have understood that Janelle and I had an episode of near intimacy, emphasis on *near*), and I would go back there again if Marie-Luce didn't have a boyfriend living there right now. Marie-Luce is a woman who is serious about love; she doesn't flit about like her sister. She takes it seriously, and I don't want to get in the way. I stay in a hotel when I go to Montreal.

What happened in that apartment almost defies understanding. Despite everything they told me – we spent hours and hours, the three of us in that apartment, Marie-Luce, Janelle, and me, going back over the story of what happened – it is hard for me to understand. How could two women of sound mind have come to such a senseless decision? How could an old woman who was dying have imposed her will on them? How could the three of them have set out on an adventure that could end only in death, believing that it was the only thing humanly possible? And then to hear from Janelle these unimaginable words, considering her abject fear of death: 'It was the most beautiful experience of my life.'

They arrived at the apartment at the beginning of the evening. Marie-Luce is a woman who is organized and plans ahead. She had prepared soup and snacks, and she had done a first pass of Janelle's bedroom. At the table, the two sisters exchanged news about friends they shared. Gladys, who was silent, dipped the back of the spoon into the thick vegetable soup to take up only the broth and, at the same time, take a pill. Which didn't escape the nurse's eye.

'Hydromorphone?' Marie-Luce asked.

Gladys nodded.

'Cancer?' ('It wasn't even a question,' Marie-Luce told me. 'I was sure of it.')

Her gaze steady, Gladys didn't answer. She knew that Marie-Luce knew.

'Lungs?'

' ... '

'Aggressive?'

' ... '

'Terminal phase?'

The questions were surgical, leaving no room for appeal. And Gladys no longer seemed concerned. Her expressionless eyes wandered over Marie-Luce.

Marie-Luce would not let herself be thrown off. Her decision was made.

'Tomorrow morning, we're taking you to the hospital.'

'No, tomorrow morning, I'm taking the train to Senne-terre. I want to die on the train.'

It was determined and delirious. They didn't believe her, this old woman delirious with fatigue. They quickly cleared the table to get Janelle's bedroom set up and put Gladys to bed. In no time, they had piled Janelle's mess at the end of the room that runs the length of the apartment and serves as the living room, kitchen, and dining room. Janelle went back to the bedroom to get Gladys's travel bag, 'I'm going to do a bit of laundry,' but Gladys was already deep in sleep.

They had the entire evening to discuss the situation and decide what was next. It was a difficult evening for Janelle, because Marie-Luce kept scolding her as she learned about her sister's foolhardy journey. Three successive trains in twenty-four hours and not for one moment did she realize she was trailing a dying woman behind her.

'My sister's life is chaos, but in her head everything is neatly arranged, properly categorized: love with love, sex with sex, money with money, and so forth. A machine that runs like clockwork. She is equipped for chaos. When she senses hassles coming that aren't hers, she packs her bags and is out of there. Somewhere else, escape, that's all Janelle knows. But this time she had stepped in a quagmire that wouldn't be that easy to get out of.'

If there was any further doubt about the quagmire they were in, they had it confirmed when Janelle set about doing 'a bit of laundry' for Gladys. At the bottom of her travel bag, they found inhalers and codeine syrup, and in her tote bag there were prescriptions for hydromorphone and fentanyl, signed by a doctor from Kirkland Lake. Everything pharmacologically required for the end of life. Gladys knew what awaited her when she left home.

And death, her fear of it, came crashing down on Janelle. Death was right there, close by, in her bed, something horrible, hideous, slimy, black, repugnant. Janelle has no memory of what Marie-Luce said to snap her out of it, 'a complete blackout,' but the image of the horror that had invaded her bed is still vivid in her mind: 'I thought I would die from Gladys's death.'

Marie-Luce is familiar with her sister's panicked fear at the idea of death but had never seen her in that state. 'The blood drained from her face before my very eyes; I wondered whether she was going to faint. I made her lie down on the sofa, her legs raised, and I rubbed her whole body to get her circulation going, and I talked and talked and talked. I explained that there was nothing to fear that night. Gladys wasn't going to die that night or the next day; she still had a few more days. We would take her to the hospital first thing the next day. They would take over, give her all the care she needed, and she would drift off peacefully. But it wasn't enough. I could tell by her terror-stricken eyes.'

A phone rang; it was Janelle's, abandoned in an armchair, a musical ringtone that filled the air and shook off the fear. Janelle quickly extricated herself from her sister to go see to her iPhone. She recognized the number from Swastika and let the phone warble. 'I was in no shape to talk to Lisana or anyone else.' The phone finally stopped ringing, and Marie-Luce asked who it was.

At that point, the evening took another turn, because hundreds of kilometres away there was a woman who also wanted to die. A woman who was living with the anticipation, obsession, and fear of the act that would set her free. At least that was how Janelle saw it. Lisana didn't want death so much as living with the idea of death. That was what Marie-Luce thought too. She wasn't all that impressed. She had seen bloodied wrists in the emergency room at the hospital. None of those men and women had managed to bleed to death. Slashing your wrists is not a guaranteed way out; you have to hit the radial artery, and Lisana had made too many attempts not to know where the radial artery is.

They were in the dining section of the room, sitting across the table from each other, a beer in front of each of them. Overwhelmed, silent, Marie-Luce got up to peek in on Gladys. When she came back, another beer was waiting for her, then another ('We almost emptied a case of twelve'), and they continued in silence a conversation that was getting them nowhere. The night was gloomy. Janelle was struggling with thoughts that were foreign to her. 'I felt like an animal caught in a trap.' She looked at the night growing deeper through the window. She would have liked to disappear into it, to stop thinking. Marie-Luce was contemplating the same night. She was unravelling a complicated tangle of thoughts and searching for the missing thread.

'Call her back,' Marie-Luce finally said. 'Your Lisana is in distress; you can't leave her like that.'

'I called her back hoping she wouldn't answer. But she picked up on the first ring, and I heard a "Mom?" that was so shrill, so alarmed, that I put the phone on speaker because I didn't want to be alone with her.'

'Your mother is sleeping. She's exhausted. She's sick,' Janelle immediately said, her voice firm. ('I didn't want to hear all the nonsense, karma and all that.')

'I know.'

'Very sick. She has cancer.'

'I know.'

'But don't worry, I'm with my sister Marie-Luce. She's a nurse.'

'I know. You already told me.' ('Her repeated *I know*s were irritating. But reassuring. I had her attention.')

'Tomorrow we're going to take her to the hospital ... here ... in Montreal. Hôpital Saint-Luc ... '

'I know. She's going to die.' ('A distant tone, as if she were announcing the weather.')

' ... '

Marie-Luce came to the rescue. She explained that they would take good care of her mother at the hospital, that it had everything she needed, that it was the best place for her under the circumstances, and she assured Lisana that they would give her daily updates about her mother's condition.

'I want to die at the same time as my mother.'

Marie-Luce didn't let her go on. She told Lisana what she wanted to hear, that it was her right, that it was her life, that no one would try to stop her. She didn't give her a pep talk about life, and Lisana, relieved not to have to sit through it, listened attentively without saying a word. Marie-Luce ended the conversation by pointing out the time, the need for all three of them to get a good night's sleep, and Lisana, in a calm, almost civil, voice, wished her a good night in turn.

The room fell silent again. All that could be heard was the snoring from Gladys's room. A gentle, steady snoring that reassured Marie-Luce about the night ahead. Gladys was sleeping peacefully. They would not have to watch over her.

Janelle wasn't in the same frame of mind. She wouldn't stop looking at the bedroom, listening for the sounds emerging from it.

'Come on,' Marie-Luce said, and she led her to the bedroom.

Gladys was sleeping a calm, tranquil sleep, sprawled beneath the covers, her face turned toward the window where street noises were coming from. As if she were breathing to the rhythm of the echoes of conversation, laughter, and the clacking of steps on the sidewalk. As if life were coming through the window to gently greet her. That was what Marie-Luce wanted Janelle to see. An old woman resting in the acceptance of death.

The sisters slept together, huddled against each other, like a single body. A dreamless night with no disruptions, without the heavy anticipation of the day that awaited them.

The day managed to advance, hour after hour, with constant tension, until a decision imposed itself and finally calmed them – that's what they tried to get me to understand. How they ended up bowing to Gladys's will. How they wound up agreeing at the end of the day to what appeared to be the only thing humanly possible. A decision in which they found strength and relief despite everything they said and did to avoid it.

Because they fought, they resisted, they did the impossible not to end up here, and now that there is no going back, they know that nothing could have resisted Gladys's will, the strength in her eyes and the accompanying smile. More than the look in her eye, it was Gladys's smile that wore them down as the hours went by. A smile that refused to yield despite every objection they offered, a smile that was already firmly in place in the morning, when she refused to go to the hospital.

'A patient, resilient smile,' Marie-Luce told me, 'as if we were suggesting going for a drive and she had a better idea.'

The train trip, Montreal–Senneterre, was what she wanted, required, demanded, with a smile directed (solely and exclusively, Marie-Luce told me) at Janelle.

The Montreal–Senneterre line, like the Budd Car but running north-south, does three return trips a week, and there is no departure for Senneterre on Sundays. 'A blessed day of all days, because it was Sunday.' They thought they had an excuse.

'Sunday? It's Sunday today?' Gladys inquired.

They thought she was confused, but they quickly understood that Gladys had a route all traced out that she would not be deviated from.

'Today is Sunday … tomorrow is Monday … We can take the train to Senneterre tomorrow morning,' Gladys finally announced, with a smile dulled from effort ('to Janelle, once again, all of her attention was on Janelle'), before asking her whether she had called Lisana, her other obsession.

It was a long day, with a lot of pressure. There was no longer a question of hospitalizing Gladys. No question either of having an old woman dying in Janelle's bed. 'It was possible; I could have given her end-of-life care, but just seeing Janelle's terrified face, I couldn't consider it.' The day dragged on.

The strangest thing, they told me, was seeing Gladys so serene, so confident. They went into the bedroom just to watch her sleep, to see the woman's beautiful, large body stretched out on the bed or curled around the pillows, like a fetus with its cord, or settled into any other position that kept her comfortable. She was taking joy in her body, in the life she had left.

The bedroom radiated the same peaceful abandon, whether or not she was sleeping. Abandon to her body, abandon to her two angels ('That's what she called us') when they would tiptoe in to give her a bite to eat, rearrange her pillows, refresh her with a cool cloth, and explain once again that she had to go to the hospital, that she was in no shape to travel, and, relaxed and smiling, she welcomed them as if they had just brought her good news, saying she was going to take the Montreal–Senneterre train the next morning.

'We didn't know how we were going to get through the day.'

The only time they saw a flash of worry in her eyes was when she asked Janelle whether she had called Lisana. But she never asked to speak to her daughter. That is what the sisters couldn't explain, not now and not then.

Janelle called Lisana twice during the day. The first time in the morning when Gladys had already fallen back into a deep sleep. Lisana was raving. Her karma, the neighbours, their eyes coming through the walls, her karma again, and then, as if she had grown tired of her own confusion, she became more coherent, wondering what she would do with her day, whether *Homeland* was on Showtime today. Janelle got the impression of organized, self-aware confusion.

The second call happened in Gladys's presence, in Janelle's bedroom, the phone on speaker. They thought that getting the mother and daughter communicating would create an emotional shock that would release each from her own obsessions.

But there was no communication and no emotional shock. Janelle carried out the conversation on her own, under Gladys's silent smile. Not one word, no reaction, just that smile, which showed her satisfaction in listening to the two women speaking. And nothing Lisana said was addressed to her mother. She was raving less, less worried about her karma, almost relaxed. Although karma came up at the end of the conversation when Janelle asked her to convince her mother to give up on the idea of making the train trip. 'My mother's karma is to die on a train,' Lisana said, and Gladys smiled in agreement.

They have no idea how the decision developed in the hours that followed.

'There was no decision. On our part, I mean. I don't remember a moment when my sister and I decided anything. The decision happened without our noticing. At the end of the afternoon, we knew we were going to take the Montreal–Senneterre train.'

'Gladys always knew, she never doubted it. She always knew I would go with her. She is a formidable woman.'

At the end of the afternoon, Marie-Luce went to the pharmacy to stock up on items for end-of-life care.

On Monday, October 1, I walked into class not realizing that my life was going to be turned upside down. Seven hundred kilometres from my classroom, three women weighed down with luggage (Marie-Luce hadn't managed to convince her sister to leave anything behind) and stunned by their own determination boarded the Montreal–Senneterre train. And farther away still, in Sudbury, Suzan and her son were starting the trip to Swastika.

I couldn't say whether it was space or time that sealed my fate or whether the two colluded against me, nor whether, in this space-time, I could have found a way to escape. I don't like the idea of destiny; I don't accept the idea that written somewhere in the sky or in my DNA there is a life that awaits me. And yet, when I think back to all the facts and everyone's acts recorded here, I can see myself putting my foot in the trap the evening of October 1, and I can't help but think that there was a misdeal. I'm not made for the whirlwind that followed.

Senneterre is a small town where nothing happens except for its forest festival and the trains pulling into and out of the station. Chance would have it that I was born there, and the days passing me by or my lack of determination have made it so that I am still there. I serve as the local dreamer. Hard work is what's valued here, and I do nothing with my hands other than turn the pages of a book, so I have been designated an intellectual. I have no illusions about the title. I have never read Baudelaire. I read fantasy, science fiction, biographies, and anything I can get my hands on about trains. History, technical manuals, life stories, the great builders, hoboes from the 1930s, ghost train hunters, it all interests me. If a sign of destiny were needed, you would find it in my passion for trains.

Why didn't I become a railwayman like my father, my uncles, and all the young men seeking a future for themselves not too far away? Probably because they were men who were larger than life in my mind. My father, who was not actually a colossus, seemed like a giant when I would see him in the marshalling yard. I would look for him among the men who would lumber between the long freight trains and, once I spotted him, I wouldn't take my eyes off him, a short man who had become a giant because he would single-handedly dismantle a train. All of his gestures, the lever he would release, the brake hoses he would separate, the movements he repeated from one car to the next, I was familiar with them, and every time it was the same rapture to see the cars separate, slide along the track, and join another train, thanks to the expert hands of my father, my uncle, all the men who performed the slow, heavy, behemoth ballet.

I don't have intelligent hands. I wouldn't know how to slip like my father under the joint hooks and in five seconds release the brake hoses. The only thing my hands are good for is turning pages, and I became an English teacher.

People call me 'broken arm' or 'broken hand.' It isn't said to be mean; it is said relatively kindly because I am still 'a local guy.' Regardless, a *broken hand* has a hard time winning the heart of 'a local woman.' They want a man who is capable of uncoupling, putting away, cutting. Unable to impress the sturdy girls from Senneterre with my page-turning abilities, I play on my bookish aura with girls who arrive from other places. I lose myself between their dreams and mine, and then, obviously, after a certain amount of time, they go back from where they came.

I don't remember the moment I became a member and then the president of the Senneterre Historical Society, which gave birth – quickly and at my initiative – to the SOS Transcontinental movement. It was naturally, almost by osmosis, that I slipped among the former railwaymen who were trying their best to return to a time when our little town was a major railway centre.

Like the Bengal tiger, like the Asian elephant, like most Northern trains, the Montreal–Senneterre line is endangered. At the Historical Society, we call it 'the Transcontinental' to give it a bit of panache and protect it from the assaults of time. That was its name when it ran from Halifax to Vancouver, with the valiant pioneers of the North aboard, entire families and their household goods, peasants who came from Central Europe with only their sheepskin jackets and the vast Canadian North they had been given to dream about. Of this mythical train, there remains only the Montreal–Senneterre section, which is, in my opinion – and you will forgive me my favouritism, my bias, my complete lack of objectivity – the most interesting, the most alive, the most attractive of the Northern trains. I have done them all, and only our line offers so much to experience and contemplate.

I won't attempt an exhaustive list here of all the charms and attractions of the Montreal–Senneterre line, but I want the potential and hypothetical reader who has followed me through these lines to know what they would be giving up if the axe were to fall on our Transcontinental.

First there is the close encounter with nature. The train crosses seven hundred kilometres of deep forest and puts all of its splendour and its pain on display. Rivers, lakes, great tranquil expanses, the earth-shaking furor of the waters, a spectacle that is constantly changing. Then the injuries, the long black tree trunks rising out of land ravaged by clear-cutting and forest fires.

But it's inside, in the only car, that you get the true Transcontinental experience. Because of its passengers. I still sometimes take the trip I know inside out just for the surprise that awaits me. It never disappoints. I know that in the little community that forms over the hours (the trip takes eleven, twelve, thirteen hours, if not more), there will be someone who will create a moment of humanity that can be produced nowhere else.

Despite what people think, the Transcontinental line crosses inhabited territory – sparsely, very sparsely, and for long stretches not at all, but still inhabited. First by Indigenous people, Atikamekw territory (two reserves, Wemotaci and Obedjiwan). Then by the intractable Parent and Clova, barely one hundred people who have chosen to live in what one could think was death throes but that has a beautiful, raw vitality. Then by all the lonely souls who smell strongly of cabins in the wood and tart wind in the resiny underbrush who board and alight without a glance at anyone. Exclusively men. Although I have seen an old woman, at least eighty years old, get off the train where a younger man was waiting for her, probably her son, and farther along, the smoke that rose up between the spruce, probably the son's cabin. Which one of them was the forest hermit? I made up a whole story around their encounter.

And then there are those who this life attracts. Fishers, hunters, and kayakers who come in by the dozens for expeditions of ten or twenty days on the Bazin and Oskélanéo rivers. Nature lovers who have their cottages equipped with solar panels and a parabolic antenna somewhere on the shore of a lake. And there are all the others who come from different worlds and who never fail to surprise me. A train buff smiling broadly because he has finally stepped onto the train that was missing from his collection. A woman who's lost, a train stray (every time I see her, she has forgotten where she has come from and where she is going). A European in search of the 'Indians' from his childhood books, whom my friend Ricky quickly spots. Ricky is Atikamekw and, for a few beers, he tells the European all the stories he wants to hear, and for a few more, the European gets to hear powwow chanting. Many of us know Ricky's game. None of us step in, not even the conductor, when Ricky is dead drunk. He lives alone in the middle of the forest, banished from his reserve, and the train is his amusement park, and those of us in the car seeing him toy with the European also find it amusing. It was one of those moments that make the Transcontinental unique.

But even with two cars chock full, the Transcontinental doesn't earn its keep. It's still around because it's an essential service. For the people of Clova who have their groceries delivered by train, for the Parent clinic that sends and receives medical supplies, for the Atikamekw who travel between reserves or who go shopping or to the hospital or to college in La Tuque or Shawinigan. For all these people, the Transcontinental is a service that — we are all aware of it — will become less and less essential now that there is a forest road that takes the same route. Right now, it's just a side road for forest trucking. But as soon as it becomes passable year-round, and it will soon, we all know that will signal the death of our Transcontinental.

I was settled in, reading my copy of *Rail Fan Canada*, when I got a call from Clova early in the evening. It was Patrice, a friend, also a big fan of the Transcontinental, informing me that an old woman was dying in Clova because she couldn't get a train to Swastika. The story was confused; it took me a while to understand what it was about and if we could take advantage of it. The old woman was going to take the Northlander to get home when the line – and I knew it for a fact, having been on the last trip of the Northlander – had been retired the day before. How the old woman could have believed she would get to Swastika via the Transcontinental, Patrice had no idea, but we both knew it was a path to follow. An old woman dies because they took away her train; it was a sledgehammer of an argument to defend our own position.

I went to the station to wait for the train and find out more. I didn't know which of the Villeneuve brothers, Claude or Jean-Pierre, was the conductor that day. When I spotted Claude coming down the footboard, I knew he was in no mood to talk. His gestures were slow and deliberat,e as if he had to displace a ton of air. The passengers got off one by one, looking like survivors. Among them, the German man, the train buff with whom I had exchanged a few words on the Northlander. His specialty was endangered trains.

I had the rails in my bones. There was no way I was going to be able to resist this story.

Where did the idea come from that Gladys would meet her maker in Clova because she had missed the Northlander? That she thought she was headed to Swastika?

From person to person, I managed to untie the knots of the confusion.

From Suzan, who as she was leaving from Sudbury called Lisana, who told her that Gladys had taken the Montreal–Senneterre train – again from Suzan who then called Frank Smarz – from Frank Smarz, who alerted the Englehart dispatcher – from the dispatcher to the rail traffic controller in Montreal – from the controller who finally reached Claude Villeneuve who was at La Tuque – from one to the other, there was enough bewilderment and haste for communication to break down.

As for the main parties concerned – by which I mean Marie-Luce and Janelle, because as far as Gladys goes, we'll never know what she was thinking – they were disoriented, utterly stunned. They were aware of the absurdity of the situation. Particularly Marie-Luce, who had never set foot on a Northern train and who, in discovering the decrepitude of the car, pictured herself in a bad film playing the role of someone she didn't know.

They had bought tickets all the way to Senneterre. It was caution on Marie-Luce's part, as she knew there was a hospital there. But in the meantime, they hadn't the slightest idea of what awaited them over the seven hundred kilometres and the hours stretched before them, except that they had to be ready for what would come. They had done what they had to do before leaving. Marie-Luce had called in sick to work, they had a well-stocked cooler, pillows, blankets, and everything that would be needed for comfort in the throes of death, which could occur anywhere, at any time. As far off as possible, Janelle hoped; in Senneterre, Marie-Luce hoped ('In the meantime, we were operational').

Janelle told me that she has never felt so alive. She was sitting close to Gladys, and she felt that every minute, every second, would be taken away from her if every one of her thoughts wasn't for Gladys. She was unaware of the scenery streaming by the window or the few travellers who had taken their seats in the car.

Gladys was showing no sign of weakness or illness, as if she had been granted clemency. She was where she wanted to be. Everything about her emitted quiet strength.

As for the conductor who presided over this stretch of the Transcontinental, I tried several times to contact him, but he slipped through my fingers for reasons that I now understand and that, as astonishing as it may seem, are of a spiritual nature. He is well known among the fraternity of conductors. He was in charge of the Toronto–Montreal line but sometimes filled in elsewhere. This meant he occasionally found himself on the Transcontinental, and the Villeneuve brothers know him well. He is Indigenous, from the Atika-mekw nation. A giant, Claude Villeneuve told me. A giant who is always smiling and a man of great humanity. Was it his great humanity that made him abandon the trains for the priesthood? It's a question that will go unanswered, like so many others, because the only time I had a semblance of a conversation with him, he ended it on the pretext that he had a mass to celebrate. My other calls went straight to voice mail. He will be missing from this story and anonymous – as he wished.

The absence of his testimony in no way compromises the rest of this story, because nothing of note happened on that stretch of the Transcontinental.

At Hervey Junction, there was a crew change. The Atikamekw conductor got off there, taking with him his precious anonymity, and Claude Villeneuve, my fellow townsman, boarded.

An aside here on the Villeneuve brothers, an institution in Senneterre. There are three of them: Jean-Pierre, Claude, and André. They have all been train conductors from a young age, Jean-Pierre and Claude on the Transcontinental and André on the freight trains. And like me, they don't feel at home with the administrative jargon of the railway. When you ask Claude what he does for a living, he answers simply that he drives trains. And in my account, I will add the title of conductor, because he does that too.

There are two engineers in the locomotive, and when his fellow crew member is at the controls, Claude slips into the passenger car and goes seat to seat, greeting the regulars and explaining to new travellers what they should keep an eye out for on the Transcontinental line. Because as of Hervey Junction, nature reveals its greatest splendours. A plummeting view of the Milieu River, the feeling of gliding along the water when crossing the Réservoir Blanc stone bridge, not to mention the majestic Saint-Maurice River, which he announces to his new passengers every time it appears.

So Claude Villeneuve, engineer and conductor, takes great care of his passengers and, among those aboard, he quickly spotted the German train buff ('I see one and I know it, even before they ask me a question'), but he didn't notice anything unusual in the double-facing seats where 'an old woman and her two daughters' were sitting.

In the double-facing seats, there was indeed nothing out of the ordinary in the three women travelling together and making quiet conversation. When Claude Villeneuve boarded the Transcontinental, Gladys was telling one of her wonderful stories about the school train.

Gladys had not said a word since the departure from Montreal. Comfortably settled into a nest of blankets and pillows, she hadn't stopped smiling, 'a Mona Lisa smile,' Janelle told me, 'an inner source,' and she closed her eyes for long periods 'as if she wanted to better savour the pleasure of being there.'

But it was something else entirely. Gladys was counting the connections of the tracks. Or trying, rather. Because there came a moment when, with a sad smile and eyes closed, she sighed: 'No clickety-clack. There is no clickety-clack.'

Obviously, they didn't get it. Marie-Luce thought it was the beginnings of delirium and wanted to take her temperature. Gladys opened her eyes upon feeling the thermometer and, seeing their frightened eyes, laughed gently. 'No, no. I'm not losing my mind. It was a memory that came back to me.' And half to reassure them, half out of her own enjoyment, she told them the story of the clickety-clacks, a story that delighted them just as it did me in the little house under the trees.

They were under the spell of the story, also relieved not to be facing the inevitable already. Gladys was relaxed and smiling, and, for a moment, they forgot what lay ahead. The tension dropped a notch, and Gladys, lulled by the swaying of the train, let herself be carried off in the stream of memories.

'I was born on a school train. Would you like me to tell you the story?'

And she told the story for almost an hour. Without a single break, with no faltering of her voice, with great care for every detail, every image that came back to her memory, a light at the back of her eyes that revealed the pleasure of reliving the blessed time when a taste for happiness was given to her on the school train.

And now I will try to record as faithfully as possible what they in turn told me.

'This story made the rounds of the school trains. It was told travelling teacher to travelling teacher, school stop to school stop, from one school train line to the next; everywhere they told the story of the miracle child from Kormak. Because a miracle is precisely what it was. The miracle of Finnish women. Do you know what a Finnish woman was? Of course you don't. A Finnish woman knew how to read and count. A Finnish woman knew that brown bread was more nutritious than white bread. A Finnish woman could set out alone into the woods with her rifle and come back with two or three hares, start a batch of beer and a load of laundry, get down on her knees and scrub the floor. You don't get cleaner than a Finnish woman's house, even when it's just a cabin in the middle of the forest.

'Luckily, it was in Kormak when I decided to leave my mother's belly. One month before the due date and during a storm that left five feet of snow on the tracks. Trains weren't moving in any direction, and it was forty degrees below zero.

'I say luckily because Kormak was a small Finnish community huddled around a sawmill. There were also a few French Canadians. And when my mother had her first contractions, what do you think my father did? He ran to the first Finnish house.

'When he came back to the car with Helmi Pillonen, the hot-water pipes had frozen and burst. I won't explain the heating system on the school trains, it's too complicated, but let me tell you that my father dreaded the thought of the pipes bursting from the cold, because the car would be unusable for a month, the time it would take to repair it, and it was terrible for the reputation of a travelling teacher.

'My mother was carried by sled to the Pillonens' sauna, and that's where I was born. All the Finnish people had saunas near their homes, even in the middle of the woods, and all Finnish women gave birth in the sauna. For the heat, for the ready hot water, for the privacy, and so as not to disrupt the household. Sometimes they gave birth alone, sometimes helped by a friend. I was born in the heat of a Finnish sauna while it was cold enough to split pipes and while my father was worrying himself sick in the Pillonens' house. Not on the school train, in a Finnish sauna. But the story took on a life of its own and, having heard it so often, it's what I say too.

'The next day, the track was cleared, and the story made the rounds that a child had been born on William Campbell's school train during the worst snowstorm ever. Lots of people came to Kormak to congratulate my mother, my father, the Pillonens, anyone and everyone who had contributed to the extraordinary, marvellous history of the school trains. You see, everyone knew about the school trains back then. They were a source of national pride; they talked about them in the newspapers. So the news of the first baby born on a school train attracted a lot of people. People from the government, people from Canadian Pacific, journalists, and even Mr. MacDougall in person, the founder of the school trains, a man my father held in great esteem. There were so many people around the Pillonens' sauna that the French Canadians of Kormak, all Catholic obviously, called it the Bethlehem manger.

'A doctor from Chapleau also came to examine us both, my mother and me, and we were declared in perfect health even though I cried the whole time. "It's normal," the doctor said. "She's spitting up, keeping nothing down," Helmi Pillonen said. "It's normal, it will pass," said the doctor. And my father let him leave because he believed more in the wisdom of a Finnish woman than a licenced doctor.

'I cried day and night. I cried until I was blue. I cried so much, my mother told me, that she would cry too. Helmi Pillonen started to believe that my mother's milk was no good, and she asked for a neighbour who was nursing to feed me too. I spit up her milk and cried even harder. It was another neighbour who had the right idea. She said: "This child is allergic to milk. You have to find another way to feed her." And the women went through their vegetable stores and fed me broth. My mother told me there were four women in the sauna when I had my first bottle of vegetable broth. "You suckled it so hard," my mother said, "your cheeks caved in, and in no time you were sleeping." The women left, and my mother finally had her first night of rest.

'We spent a week in the Pillonens' sauna, my mother and me. I sucked back bottle after bottle. They gradually added meat broth to the vegetable broth. That is the miracle of Finnish women.

'And my father, who had also witnessed the drama of the crying and the miracle of the broth, decided to name me Gladys. "She will be called Gladys," he told my mother. "She will be happy and will never cry her whole life."

'So far, I have been faithful to my name, and I won't make a liar of my father today or tomorrow. Don't worry about me. There won't be any crying, any wailing. I will go quietly.'

They had passed Shawinigan without noticing the arrival of new passengers or the crew change in Hervey Junction. Gladys's story had lulled them, calmed them, practically released them from the clutches of anxiety. 'It was almost as if we were expecting a miracle too,' Janelle told me.

A mother recounting her childhood memories to her daughters, Claude Villeneuve thought, when he took over in Hervey Junction. 'The mother is a little tired, and the two daughters are very attentive.' Those were his first impressions.

It was near La Tuque that he received the first call on the radio. Nothing alarming. They were just asking him to confirm that he had aboard *the woman from Swastika*, an older woman named Gladys Comeau. Claude said he did, and as no one asked anything more, he returned to his other travellers. Who were now numerous because a large group of Atikamekw passengers had boarded in La Tuque.

They had passed Parent when Claude received the second radio call. This time, it was urgent. The rail traffic controller was forwarding him a message passed from Swastika to Englehart to Montreal, asking the conductor of the Transcontinental to make sure that *the woman from Swastika* had emergency care.

The chain of calls that ended up reaching Claude Ville-neuve came originally from Frank Smarz. There was panic in Swastika. A needless panic, according to Frank Smarz, Suzan's ramblings notwithstanding. Since the previous day, he told me, she had been burning up the phone lines with fantasies you couldn't make heads or tails of and trying to drag him into the same waters. This is why he didn't *bother* – he emphasized the expression – when he saw her on Avenue Conroy with her son.

Suzan and Desmond didn't need a crowbar. Lisana opened the door even before they had knocked. Desmond went in with his mother's suitcase and hurried off. 'There was something in that house that didn't want me there.'

When we had this conversation a few years later in Sudbury, he still hadn't managed to put words to his sense of unease. 'Probably a survival instinct. There was a dark joy in Lisana's eyes and a horrible racket in the house.'

The racket was back. After the silence that had so affected Frank Smarz during the days he went over to check the taps, the deafening cacophony from every last shouting device in the house was back. Suzan wasn't concerned. She knew Lisana's habits. But she still asked her to turn down the television, and that's when Lisana made, in a triumphant voice, an announcement, which Suzan first refused to believe but which gradually sunk in as Lisana revealed the horrible thing that both delighted and terrorized her. 'Mom and I are going to die together.' And she explained the pact they had made.

Suzan believed it; her dark instinct believed it. In that moment and during the hours when she raced about setting things in motion to undo the pact, she truly believed that Gladys had abandoned her daughter with the promise that they would both die, together and apart, as was their desire. It was absurd, she now agrees, but in the moment and in the haste of what Lisana had just told her (cancer, massive, aggressive, announced a month earlier), she truly believed that Gladys had headed off on the train, leaving her daughter the ultimate freedom to die as she wished. 'But I'm not capable of it anymore,' Lisana said, offering up a wrist that showed a latticework of old scars, with no purple trace of recent laceration.

Frank Smarz believed none of it. He had noticed that Gladys had seemed less energetic lately, less lively, and the house wasn't being kept as well. But terminal cancer, that he wouldn't have missed. As for the horrendous pact, it didn't even merit thinking about. 'Pure fantasy,' Frank Smarz said for Lisana's benefit, and, glancing at her wrist, he added: 'Some sorrows just evaporate, apparently.' Pure mean-spiritedness that Suzan put down to the 'enormous stupidity' of that man.

While all of this now seems to her to be unbelievably absurd, Suzan feels like she had slipped into a reality that always escaped her. Something between the mother and daughter she had always been excluded from. That same thing that had held them together for all those years and that allowed them to part one morning in September with no tears or heartbreak, almost with delight, if one were to believe the tone Lisana used in announcing that they were going to die *together and apart*. A suicide pact. Lisana believed it or wanted to believe it, but Gladys? What had she said to her daughter that morning that allowed them to part on such a promise? If there had been a promise, obviously.

The question is enough to swallow you up. It churns endlessly in my head. I have nothing to enlighten me, except

Suzan's dark instinct and the nameless thing she sensed the presence of. At the other end of the spectrum, there was Gladys's instinct for life, the unflagging optimism that had always kept her on the sunny side of life. That is what my friend Bernie tells me and repeats whenever I ask him the question. 'That woman was born on the sunny side of life.' He considers a thought that has not yet taken shape. I sense he is occupied by an idea that just won't come. Snippets of it get away from him sometimes, and I write them down. 'Surrender is not in the plans for that woman. She could paddle with a twig.' Cryptic sentences that don't help my own thinking.

All of this was just ramblings and fantasy, according to Frank Smarz. If it had been up to him, he never would have placed that emergency call that made its way to Claude Villeneuve.

Claude had received a call about a runaway a few years earlier. The girl ('thirteen, tops') had got on the train in Montreal. Claude had spotted her among his passengers and had immediately alerted the Sureté du Québec, who picked her up at the Senneterre station. The story had a happy ending.

He did not anticipate having another runaway on his hands. The old woman was in bad shape, he realized later. After the Atikamekw group got off at Wemotaci and another group of travellers at Parent, all that remained was a small group of around ten passengers, and in the calm that was restored, the coughing fits filled the space. It was bothering the passengers. The fits wouldn't stop, with loud breathing, almost a moan. In the car, people exchanged questioning looks and didn't dare speak. He himself wondered whether it —wouldn't be better to let them off, the woman and her daughters, in Parent, where there is a clinic and a highly skilled nurse (Anna, who was often aboard) who would know how to take care of the old woman. But they had just passed Parent.

Before joining the other engineer, he stopped in front of the double-facing seats. The old woman, between coughing and dozing, feebly tapped the thigh of what appeared to be the younger daughter – a mother and her daughters is what he had believed all along – while the other was refreshing her face with a wipe. The younger one, completely absorbed by her mother, didn't even notice him, while the other daughter hastily reassured him. 'It's fine. I'm a nurse.'

He went back to the locomotive with all that the eyes of

the woman, *the nurse*, did not tell him. 'I was not reassured, not at all.' So he didn't doubt the urgency of the situation when he received the second call about *the woman from Swastika*. He went back to the car immediately.

The atmosphere had grown heavy; the air had thinned. From one end of the car to the other, there was a palpable sense of discomfort. Not one word, not one gesture – the passengers were paralyzed, Claude told me. 'They felt threatened by what was going on in the double-facing seats.'

The situation had gotten worse. Gladys was breathing in raspy, wheezing fits and starts despite the inhaler Janelle was holding to her mouth. She was shivering under the blankets. Marie-Luce was massaging her feet and her legs. 'We were wondering whether what we were dreading had arrived.'

Claude was also afraid death would leave an indelible stain on his train. 'In thirty years of service, it had never happened to me. I didn't want a tragedy on my train. I didn't want to go on to my retirement trailing a body with chattering teeth behind me.'

They were approaching Clova, where there was no clinic, no emergency service. They had to hope the old woman would make it as far as Senneterre. That's what he asked Marie-Luce. 'There is a hospital in Senneterre. Do you think she can make it that far?' He regretted his question, because the old woman roused herself and launched into a litany of denials, the same words coming back like a heartbeat, 'No hospital … no hospital … no hospital.' Her daughters, resigned and conciliatory, repeated the words back to her, 'No hospital, okay, Gladys, understood, no hospital,' and the older one, *the nurse*, Marie-Luce, wanting to convey that they had the situation in hand, turned to Claude and told him in a flat voice, 'Don't worry, we have everything we need.' Claude wasn't reassured. He insisted. 'We're arriving in Clova; if we pick up the pace, we will be in Senneterre in two hours. Would that be okay?'

It was the word *Clova* that precipitated everything, left no further option, sealed their fate. She had barely heard the word when Gladys, in a single motion, got up from her seat and said, as if she had just discovered her destination, 'Clova, this is where we are getting off, this is where it ends for me.'

Nothing could stop her; Claude, Marie-Luce, Janelle all knew it, and they all told me so in trying to convince me that you could not go against Gladys's will.

They collected their bags and Gladys her strength and, under the astounded gazes of the travellers and Claude, who thought the old woman was drawing her last breath, Gladys walked straight and with no one's help down the aisle of the Transcontinental.

'A queen,' Janelle told me. 'She left like a queen.'

Gladys brought her eight-day journey to an end.

I know the little community of Clova, and I am not surprised that they let visitors lock themselves away in a room for days without growing alarmed or intervening in some way. If there is one thing people in Clova prize, it's freedom. *Live and let live* is the local credo. Even if in this case it was *Live and let die.* The old woman who arrived there via the Transcontinental collapsed on the outdoor bench at the Restaurant Clova, exhaling all the air from her lungs, like a whale run aground on a sandbar. The woman was at the end of the line, and no one thought they should notify anyone. You get here on your own steam, and you leave the same way.

I first need to explain the Restaurant Clova, because it is an important site that bears witness. That is where I sat down with the idea of mounting a case against the railway companies who let an old woman die along with the Northern trains. Nothing very thorough, just a few pages, but resonant, that would alert those whom it may concern. I had no idea that years would go by, pages would accumulate, and I would still be at my keyboard wondering what to do with all this clutter. At times I felt like I was writing a long letter to myself.

So, the Restaurant Clova.

The place could seem absurd, an aberration set just metres from the railway tracks with nothing around it but scattered homes and a great, still calm. And yet, at the end of the day, pickups and ATVs arrive. Men descend from them. A few women. They live around the lake, the amber waters of which can be spotted from there. They come from the surrounding outfitters. They almost all know one another. And at the end of the afternoon, many of them leave their lake or their forest and come to socialize at the Restaurant Clova. They have a drink at the bar, take a seat at a table in the restaurant section (their pizza is delicious), and if it's Monday, Wednesday, or Friday, they wait for the 5:20 train that will arrive hours late.

I understand that travellers from Montreal may think it's a gathering of hillbillies. A scene from a Western. The restaurant is a low building, not entirely ugly, and a very dark red. It's the porch with the short canopy roof that makes it look like a Western. It has two long wooden benches where people wait for the train. No matter whether they're waiting for mail, a package, a friend, or clients for the outfitter, on and around the porch there will be around fifteen people who have come to witness the event that is the arrival of the train. Beside it, close by, the little station that has sat idle for years has become part of the scenery, almost a commemorative ornament from the time when Clova was a major railway stop. The station is charming, with its hipped roof, dormer windows, and cornices.

I arrived in Clova on October 2. Janelle and Marie-Luce had been there since the day before, shut up with Gladys in a room at the inn. I was staying with my friend Patrice and eating at the restaurant. Coffee after coffee, I whiled away the hours, hoping to see someone arrive from the inn. From there I could watch the comings and goings of everyone who was rushing to Gladys's bedside.

Suzan and Lisana had arrived in the morning on the train from Senneterre. Frank Smarz and his wife, Brenda, arrived the next day in their pickup truck. They were all staying at the inn, and they came to the restaurant, each on their own schedule, sometimes alone, sometimes in twos, rarely in threes. I would see them pick at their meals, and I wondered how I could make an initial approach. There was such silence at their table.

There is nothing better than a smoker in need to attract attention. At the end of a meal, I saw Frank Smarz reach for his jean jacket pocket, then go to the bar, come back empty-handed, and I blessed the day I started to smoke again. I got up to offer him a cigarette, and we found ourselves on the porch, two smoking pariahs who had no choice but to talk to each other. This is how I learned the whole story, or at least its substance.

Janelle appeared in the evening when young people and old loners descend on the restaurant. The restaurant becomes a bar, and the porch becomes a pot den. It could have been any bar in Montreal, if it weren't for the confident patrons' nonchalance and the complete lack of concern about dress. The youngest ones are employees of the outfitters in the area. As for the older ones, some of them have come to hide in Clova. Hide from what, no one knows, and no one wants to know.

Janelle appeared, and I already knew both that she wasn't for me and that I would not escape her. I know how to spot in myself my shock when faced with a woman I will pursue for the smell of her skin, her breath in the morning, her eyes rolling back in her head, until our fireworks end. An elusive woman, who comes out of nowhere, who looks like no one I've ever seen. I don't fall in love with my cousin. And Janelle is a sort of UFO. A woman who bursts into your life and who sears you clear through. When she appeared in the door of the restaurant, I felt it in my whole body.

There was an abrupt dissonance in her gestures and eyes that I think I've described, and a way of moving, somewhere between disjointed steps and the undulations of a dancer, which is not without its charm. I was on alert, disoriented, turned to stone. Which in me is the sign of an impending lightning bolt of love. I never resist it, despite what it will cost me, which I already know. I watched her head to the bar. She sat down, ordered a beer, and started a long conversation with the waitress – tattoos, piercings, half-shaved head; she wouldn't look out of place on Rue Saint-Denis. I took the opportunity to slip to her side. I tried several times to insert myself in the conversation, but every time she gave me the cold shoulder. Later, when we established the intimacy that she was quick to slip away from, she explained that she thought she was dealing with the internet beau. 'I didn't want anything to do with it anymore, and anyway, quite often, these guys try to put one over on you with their photos.'

That was our first contact, the only one for three long days. I didn't see her again at the restaurant until they all gathered there in a sort of funeral meal. And that was when I saw Marie-Luce for the first time. She had stayed at Gladys's bedside all those days, with someone from the group bringing her meals from the restaurant.

The person I saw most often and with whom I was able to have actual conversations was Suzan. She went for long walks in the sandy streets of Clova, going wherever they led and stopping at the restaurant for a coffee break before going back to the inn. Probably because she is old and lives in proximity to death, there was no sense of impending mourning in her. On the contrary, she told me. She was relieved that mother and daughter were finally reunited.

Lisana, what can I say about the Lisana I met in Clova? Silent, absolutely impenetrable, and yet a presence that could not be ignored. She walked into the restaurant and there was a vibration in the air. But no one turned when she walked by. People are used to strangers in Clova. They come from all over for the fishing, the hunting, for whatever they are after, and people don't ask questions. They see them come and go, others will arrive, and they are welcomed with the same graciousness, the same detachment. The residents don't bother about who they are, what they've come to do. A supreme indifference that cracked in the presence of Lisana. Nothing obvious, just a slight disquiet that my focused attention noticed immediately because I was on alert whenever someone arrived from the inn.

Yet there was nothing in her appearance that set her apart from the other women who frequented the place. Jeans, running shoes, a fleece jacket, and hair carefully gathered in a nice, smooth ponytail. ('I made sure of it,' Suzan told me later. 'I wanted her to be a credit to her mother.') Nor did she have that lost, troubled look they would tell me about in Swastika. A mass of contained energy, that's what she was, energy that spread in sustained vibrations.

She came to the restaurant with Suzan. Never, except for the funeral meal, did I see her sit down at a table with the Smarzes. And I never saw the headphones that so intrigued me during the investigation. In fact, there was nothing that would attract attention if it weren't for the tremendous energy she emitted. And no one from the group at the inn mentioned any mental health problems. Not even Suzan, who was rather chatty when she would come back from her walks.

These people who are now part of my life, I met them at the Restaurant Clova. Only Gladys remained a stranger, out of reach, shut away as she was in a little room at the inn. But daily, almost hourly, I got news of what was going on at the inn, thanks to Frank Smarz (he was a heavy smoker, and I was his supplier) and Suzan, whom I would sometimes accompany on her walks. I didn't know at the time that these moments spent together in Clova would be the prelude to long conversations we would have later in Metagama.

She is a personable woman, curious about others, who doesn't make a mystery out of life. Our conversations headed off in every direction but, as soon as the words *school train* came up, I would jump on the slightest remark to come back to it. It was so fabulous; I could hardly believe that I had never heard the story. I have piles of books on my bookshelves about trains, but none of them mention it. Suzan opened the door to a new world for me, and I already knew it would never cease to intrigue me. Suzan herself was a world to discover. An old woman who lived like a hermit along the railway tracks. 'Semi-hermit,' she pointed out. I still knew nothing about the possibilities for contemplation offered by the clickety-clacks.

Calm and serene, she was more inclined to talk to me about what she had seen on her solitary walks through the streets of Clova than what was going on at the inn. She had not ventured beyond the church that now serves as a shed for the couple that lives in the presbytery. Beyond the church, there is what remains of the large village Clova once was, an enclave of houses abandoned to the forest. She didn't know about the ghost village. In fact, no one in Clova gives it any thought. I know the place well. I go there sometimes when I want to travel through time, to wander around what once was and is no longer. There is always a surprise waiting for me. A carmine red patch in the middle of the wild grass, flowers I don't know the name of, that stubbornly live on without the woman who planted them, watered them, carefully weeded around them, and I think of that woman, of what she lived through in a house that must have been close to the red patch and of which nothing remains, not even a cement block eroded by weather. I have discovered papers forgotten in a dresser, children's scribbles, bills, letters to a parent far away. I love these walks, nostalgic for a time I never knew that I like to imagine. But sometimes it's incredibly sad. I offered to take Suzan there.

The ghost village had shrunk since my last visit. There were no more than five houses left, so dilapidated that we didn't dare go in any of them for fear that the floor would give out under our weight. Through the windows, we saw collapsed ceilings, sinks torn off the wall, gutted sofas, and, what surprised Suzan, beer cans all over the floor. Atikamekw youth, I explained. They don't feel welcome at the bar.

Our visit to old Clova was short. We walked along what used to be the streets and that are clearly used only by ATVs and the rare walker, like us.

It was once we had returned from the ghost village that she told me about the cemetery in Clova, 'the prettiest little cemetery in the world.' I didn't know it, had never been. Suzan discovered it by chance on her walks by following the sand road that runs along the lake. You really have to want to see it all to get there. No signs, no path going there except for ATV trails criss-crossing in the woods, and, if you follow the one that goes up a hill, you can see a clearing in the forest that is indeed a little jewel of a cemetery. And there, still, there is nothing to make it official. A chain with large white links that hangs around a mossy square, wooden crosses, modest headstones, some thirty graves set against a backdrop of greenery. The impression of a secret place, of being at the centre of the beauty of the world. The light that slips between birch and the amber waters of the lake below add to the gentleness of the place. 'A nice place to watch eternity go by,' Suzan said.

I explained to her that no one dies in Clova anymore, that the little cemetery is a vestige of a not-so-distant past when Clova had a population of six hundred. There are now no more than thirty-odd people who live there permanently, most of them retirees who have come from other places, attracted by the beauty of the lake and the low cost of living, and they will die back where they come from.

But we knew, both knew with certainty, that there would be a death in Clova very soon. 'I think it will be tomorrow,' Suzan said.

It was Wednesday, October 3. Gladys died the next day, just as the freight train was pulling into Clova, making the earth tremble.

It would take Gladys four days to reach the end – and her ends, because no one now doubts they were gathered together where she wanted them. Four days, and at no time did they feel exasperated or despairing about the death that was long in coming. She waited with them, confident despite the hours and days that passed, no resistance other than that smile that slowly returned as she emerged from deep, comatose sleep. She accompanied them throughout, captain of her life until the very last.

They were living in a bubble. They were the only guests at the inn, occupying the five rooms on the ground floor. They lived in the unreality of days and nights spent at Gladys's bedside in a downy cocoon, a sort of floating. They have gentle, gratifying memories of it. Even Frank Smarz, who is not a man easily moved wherever the wind blows, talked about a sort of grace they had been offered.

This floating that was with them in their steps and their thoughts came from Gladys's room. No haste, no muffled conversations when approaching her room, they went weightlessly, drawn by the call of her smile or, if the hydromorphone was taking effect, by the peaceful abandon of her body in the bed. The soft, cozy room, like the room of a newborn, spread its silken threads throughout the inn. In the hallway, the rooms, and the spacious lounge in the basement. The inn is the former Clova school, and what is now a lounge used to be the games room. And that's where they spent most of their time. Waiting for what was taking its time coming. They played cards, watched TV, distractedly, half-heartedly, their attention consumed by what was going on upstairs.

They no longer had to worry about anything, there were no more calls to make or receive, no more flurry of train schedules. They just had to be there, with nothing to do but wait.

Marie-Luce was relieved to see them arrive one by one. She hadn't left Gladys's side since settling her into the little room at the inn. Janelle was trying to help her as best she could, but it was beyond her. She would leave the room at the first signs of Gladys nodding off and would go get some air, never very far, because Gladys would ask for her as soon as she woke. Janelle would come back, sit on the edge of the bed, take Gladys's outstretched hand, and, even before Gladys had asked the question, she would repeat what she had said an hour before, two hours before, every hour since they had arrived in Clova. 'Yes, Gladys, yes, I called her. Yes, she's coming.' And Gladys's patting … 'My Lisana isn't easy to love, but you'll see, you're going to love her.'

Lisana's arrival was a liberation and a source of astonishment. They expected the agitation of a storm, and what they saw arriving was a rock, a woman whose emotions had turned to stone.

Even Suzan was surprised at what Lisana became in her mother's presence. Gladys was sleeping the peaceful, deep sleep that wrapped the room in a downy cocoon. Lisana, erect and immobile near the bed, watched her mother sleep. Not one move, not one word, she was absorbed by her mother's breathing, her bony face, her shrunken body; death was doing its work. Lisana became a woman of a completely difference stature, 'a giant,' Suzan told me. She took up all the space in the room. Her mother probably sensed her presence because she woke up and looked at her daughter. 'You came,' she said simply, and Lisana acquiesced, 'I came,' and their eyes melted into the other's, merged, disappeared into each other while they chatted.

Suzan was alone with them in the room, Marie-Luce having disappeared at their arrival. They had driven at night from Swastika to Senneterre to take the train for Clova early in the morning. Suzan was exhausted from the trip. She got a second wind when she arrived in the room, buffeted by the intensity of what was going on; then, overcome by fatigue, she collapsed into the only armchair the small room allowed.

'The Toyota held up?' Gladys, tucked deep in her bed, with shining eyes and a sidelong smile, was asking for news of her car. Suzan approached, and the two old friends talked about this and that, the road from Metagama, the road from Swastika, but nothing about her own trip, her journey on the rails, and one thing led to another, they got to her health, whether she was in pain ('Just enough to feel alive'), if she was afraid ('Afraid of what, good Lord, I've made it this far'), until Gladys asked them to fetch Janelle.

'We made the trip by car and by train, mostly at night, to be there, me and Lisana, at her side, and she was asking for a woman she hardly knew … You have to admit, there's reason to be put off.'

You don't refuse a dying woman, and despite herself Janelle found herself back in the room she had been trying to get away from. Gladys greeted her with a long, languid smile, and she made a gesture Janelle knew well ('She patted the covers',) asking her to come over to the bed, across from Lisana. Which she did almost on tiptoe, feeling as if she were walking on a burning rug. Once they were both at her side, Gladys looked at one, then the other, and then one then the other again, her smile growing wider, growing brighter, bringing the two women together, her daughter and the one who had brought her daughter to her, with the same blissful satisfaction. 'My daughter Lisana,' she said to one. And to the other, 'My friend Janelle.' Adding with a voice that was nothing more than a wisp, 'You could be sisters.' She brought their two hands together and placed hers on top. Then, out of strength, her head dropped back on the pillow. Marie-Luce was called to the rescue.

The Smarzes arrived at the end of the day. The group that was going to accompany Gladys in the final hours of her life was complete. The inn was set for a vigil. Marie-Luce acted as steward. She decided who was on watch when, monitored medication and general comfort; she was the go-to person day and night.

Frank Smarz, the only man in the group, took care of supplies, which included the meals he brought from the restaurant, and the beer, chips, and sundry items he found in the same place, because the restaurant was equipped with a cubbyhole that served as a convenience and liquor store. It was a role that suited him perfectly. He remained in the action but was exempt from his turn on watch. He wouldn't have been able to stand it. 'Sitting there in front of a woman who is dying isn't my thing.' We would meet up at regular intervals on the restaurant porch.

Time became elastic, it had no more substance, even for me who was monitoring from afar what was going on at the inn via trustworthy, detailed reports from Frank Smarz about how the death throes were progressing. But I found out about the strange intimacy with death that gently descended upon Gladys's room much later from Suzan, Janelle, Marie-Luce, and Brenda (we mustn't forget Brenda, even though once again she found herself on the fringes of that intimacy, the poor thing).

Time concentrated around Gladys. Her breathing, her face buried in the pillow, her shining eyes that were growing dimmer, the rictus that was dulling her smile, the pain that came back, and Lisana almost always at her mother's side.

Lisana standing near the bed, not moving, ramrod straight. Lisana grown larger by emotion, but impassive, smooth, like marble. Lisana who was never left alone with her because she was useless at offering care.

'She was finally seeing death, which she had been calling for so long. She was living it through her mother.'

A contemplation of death, is what Suzan understood in those long hours of Lisana's sentry duty in Gladys's bedroom.

'She was contemplating death, which was taking hold of her mother.'

Suzan believes that it was during all those hours watching the gradual march of death that her fascination with it evaporated. 'There was no more mystery. Death was there, visible, palpable. Death had laboured breathing, death smelled like medication, death was shrivelled up in the bed. There were no more dark tunnels, no more twilight to cross, nothing to see on the other side, only life leaving a body. Her desire to die died with her mother.'

Suzan understood nothing of Gladys's insistence at having Janelle at her side too.

The scene was repeated regularly, almost a constant. Gladys would ask for Janelle, and when she had them both by her side, despite the exhaustion and weakness that left her so little voice in the final days, she would say their names, she would call them from the well of her strength, and what with her confusion (or a wilful confusion, Suzan wondered), she would mix up their names, saying Lisana when speaking to Janelle and Janelle when looking at her daughter. With the same tenderness and the same affection in her eyes and her voice. Then, when she was soothed, reassured, her smile would spread, her body would settle into the bed, and she would sleep deeply.

The most astonishing thing was that Janelle stayed. She didn't leave the room. She who was horrified by death stayed with Lisana until Gladys would moan, grimace in pain, or choke on her secretions. In which case she would call Marie-Luce, who would come right away.

On the morning of the fourth day, Gladys said: 'Today I want to sleep a lot.' Marie-Luce increased the doses of hydromorphone and fentanyl.

As the hours went by, her breathing grew lighter, her hands turned blue, life deserted her while she was submerged in a deep sleep. At the beginning of the afternoon, they all met in the little room. There was a moment when she was aware of their presence. She wanted to smile (at least, that's what they believed), but she didn't have the strength.

The freight train pulled into Clova. They heard the whistle, the hammering of the rails; then, in the crowded room, a voice was heard, 'sixteen … eighteen … twenty … thirty-two … sixty … one hundred and four …'

'Gladys died on the one hundred and thirty-eighth clickety-clack,' Suzan said.

'Her face was peaceful, at rest, her features relaxed, nothing moved under the skin of her face and yet it seemed as though the smile was still there, that she was smiling at me, that she was still there in the room, and I felt at one with what was around me, the walls, the bed, the smell, all of us gathered in the gentle feeling of that room. I felt a quiver on my lips; I don't know whether I smiled, but I know that I was at peace with myself. The most beautiful moment of my life,' Janelle said.

But there was no clickety-clack to be heard where they were or anywhere else in Clova. The rail junctions on this stretch of track are no longer made up of splice bars and bolts; they are welded every 140 feet. You no longer hear that sound characteristic of a train moving over the rail junctions, the clickety-clack so dear to Gladys's heart and that Suzan intoned so that her friend could die accompanied by her childhood memories.

I stayed in Clova for a few more days. I had everything I needed to write up my report. But I stayed there, not really knowing what was holding me, the woman who was so expertly ignoring me and who I was tracking in my thoughts, or the obsession that had taken hold, the school trains, ever since Suzan had told me about them during our walks. I came and went between the restaurant and Patrice's house, where he welcomed me with his invariable and inevitable 'So?' casually tossed off but that was no less a question. 'So?' was what was going on at the inn, it was my progress with Janelle, and, what interested him the most, because he had been bitten too, whether I had managed to get more information about the school trains. And he would tell me in turn what he had discovered during my absence.

Because Patrice has boundless curiosity. You talk to him about something, an unusual fact, a piece of trivia, and if there is something unfamiliar or unclear to him, he will go straight to his computer. He is an odd character. His presence in this almost non-existent place fuels the rumour that people come here to be forgotten. No one in Clova understood why he moved into his brother's house after his death. Patrice has no troubled past or great sorrow dogging him. He is a bookseller, a book lover who has a bookstore on AbeBooks, a website for rare and used books. When his brother died, he closed up shop in Montreal and moved his bookstore to the little house on the lake, and from the privacy of this place he engages – daily, lovingly, passionately, hungrily – with the world.

The school train story obviously intrigued him, and he googled everything he could. There was very little; the internet has only snippets of information to offer, but enough to fuel a budding obsession.

So I stayed in Clova for two days after Gladys's death, without knowing what I was doing there. Later, I thought of Léonard Mostin, left to his own devices in a virtually non-existent place also with something to write, much more substantial than my little report, and who was wondering whether life had played a trick on him.

I got nothing out of Suzan regarding the school trains during those two days. She was much too busy (the coroner who came from La Tuque, having the remains transported to Swastika, announcing the death of their sister to the Campbell siblings, etc.) to resume our conversations. The little group at the inn splintered as the days went by. Brenda and Frank Smarz headed back to Swastika on Saturday. Marie-Luce went back to Montreal on the Sunday Transcontinental. Alone, without Janelle. I realized that only later, there are such crowds on Sunday when the Transcontinental pulls in.

Janelle, whose every millimetre of skin I had roamed during the endless nights dreaming of her on Patrice's sofa, Janelle, whose presence I felt no matter where she was, Janelle, central to my thoughts day and night, Janelle had gotten away from me. I had not seen her board the Transcontinental with her sister and then get off.

On Sunday morning, the residents of Clova come to pick up their provisions for the week that arrive from Senneterre. I helped Patrice with his grocery boxes. Patrice doesn't have a pickup or an ATV (another oddity that makes him suspect in Clova), and we loaded up his boxes on the Nath Express, a massive ATV with storage space in the back, which serves as a taxi. It was only after loading up the last box that astonishment in Patrice's eyes caused my own to look toward the three women, Suzan, Lisana, and Janelle, on a bench on the porch of the restaurant.

Once we had that sort of intimacy that I can't quite define and that included conflagrations in bed and the conversations that would follow, she told me about her own astonishment at finding herself there: 'I knew I was taking on Lisana. Maybe I always knew, despite myself. But I knew it for certain when Gladys introduced me to Lisana and joined our two hands. There was nothing to do, nothing to say. You don't go against the wishes of a dying woman. But what awaited me on the other side of that wish was shrouded in darkness. I was there, on the bench, utterly stunned.'

She took the Transcontinental the next day with Suzan and Lisana. Direction Senneterre and then Swastika.

I was to leave that day for my Monday classes. A colleague had agreed to fill in if I promised to be back on Monday morning.

I ate at the restaurant before hitting the road. All three of them were there. Suzan, Lisana, and Janelle. At the end of the meal, I went to say goodbye to them. Suzan was cordial, Lisana didn't say a word, didn't even look at me, and Janelle, courteous, almost friendly, asked about the kilometres I had to travel, the road conditions, the model of my pickup, which surprised me coming from her. Even more astonishing, she got up from the table, and walking me to the door, she told me with the same civility, the same detachment, as if we were still talking about my pickup: 'Anyway, we wouldn't have lasted.'

I drove the 250 kilometres as light as a bird returning to its nest. She had sensed me, she had seen me circling her, I existed for her.

B ack home, I had awaiting me my report, which didn't want to be written. It was so short, a few pages, a speck of dust, but each time I sat down to it, the speck of dust would kick up in a thick cloud. A Hydra with a thousand heads appeared as soon as I typed the first word. I hazily knew that what lay ahead was too vast to be contained in a few pages, and I would spend hours in front of my blinking cursor, awaiting the second word.

From time to time I would receive an email from Patrice asking me how it was going, whether I would soon be reading VIA Rail the riot act, whether I was going to make them understand that the survival of the Northern trains was a matter of life and death. More than anyone in Clova, he needs the Transcontinental. He ships his book orders by train. The disappearance of the Transcontinental would mean more than the end of his small business: his entire life would fall apart. He found in AbeBooks the freedom he didn't have when he ran a store in Montreal. No more waiting for customers, no more redoing his store window, no more accounting, nothing to distract from his true passion. He just has to write up descriptions, put them online, respond to orders, ship the books, and every month he receives a cheque from AbeBooks. He always has his nose in a book. Novels, poetry, travel writing, it doesn't matter. With a predilection for books that interest no one but the person who has been looking for them for years – literary treatise, obsolete grammar manual, handbook of a lost art – and who wants to know where and how he made such a marvellous find. Patrice has email correspondences that have been going on for years with customers around the world. These exchanges are the spice of his life.

He is the one who found for me *The Bell and the Book*, a book that covers twenty-seven years of life on the school trains. Andrew Donald Clement, the author, a travelling teacher, has practically become a friend. So have the Wrights, Helen and Bill, whose correspondence (1928–1964) I read, a rare, unpublished document (I read it on CD), carefully preserved by the Chapleau municipal library, unearthed by Patrice after days – and nights, I'm convinced – of online research. Their correspondence is brimming with epic, amusing details about daily life on a school train. Helen Wright's ice cream recipe (lard and evaporated milk) is a thing of brilliance. And obviously I read *School on Wheels*, a booklet in honour of Fred Sloman (forty years on the Capreol–Foleyet line), the most recognizable figure of a bygone world.

My cursor continued to blink without me. I was fascinated, awed by the books, which I would read and reread. I couldn't sit down to write my report while there was this fascinating world drawing me in. And what seemed extraordinary about it was that a humble little English teacher in a humble little town had spent time not long before with a person from that world.

I thought I had forgotten Janelle and the shaking earth when Patrice announced to me by phone that she had returned to Clova. And without knowing whether it was really her who was drawing me back there or what she could tell me about Suzan's and Gladys's lives on the school trains, I headed back to Clova.

I knew I had gone there for her when I saw her behind the bar. Two months had gone by, it was December, a Saturday night, and the place was packed. Snowmobile season had just started, and people came from all over.

They had driven hundreds of kilometres through laby-
rinths of snow, snowmobilers arriving in backfiring hordes
at the Restaurant Clova.

I saw surprise in her eyes, and a twinkle of amusement,
then a flash of pleasure in seeing me at the end of the bar. I
was reassured. She served the long line of snowmobilers,
quick and efficient, a simple 'What'll you have?', moving to
the next customer, and when she came to me, she asked:
'What's your name?' Bingo!

I don't know what to call what happened between us.
Love? It's such a fickle word, so sensitive. It wants, then
doesn't want, to be named, wants for a time, then tires of
itself, would like to but it gets complicated, and complicated
is what things got between Janelle and me. Did I mention
that we travelled to Paris together to meet Léonard Mostin?
I don't think so, I don't know, I don't reread what I've written.

We never had true intimacy, laying ourselves bare, which
involves much more than going to bed – which we did with
fervour and devotion, but without me laying a finger on
Janelle's secret depths. Janelle does not reveal herself, does
not surrender; she never showed me the divine path to a
truly romantic relationship, the inner receptacle that holds
a person's intimate feelings that you open in the surrender
of lovemaking.

It's true that our relationship was warped from the beginning by the whole story (Gladys, Lisana, Suzan, the school
trains) to which she now held several keys and that she would
tell me about night after night, day after day, and that served
as her shield, because I never tired of it and there was always
something to tell.

She had spent more than two months in Swastika. Why
had she followed Suzan and Lisana? It was the only thing
she could do, she told me. There was a voice inside her telling

her that was what she should do. 'I now know it was in Chapleau, when she saw me in the Budd Car, that I was chosen. She knew she had found the person who would accompany her to the end, and at the end, there was Lisana.'

She would hear Gladys's voice everywhere in Swastika. She would go into the streets, to the park, to the station promontory, and she would hear Gladys telling her that she was on the right path, that she was going to find what she hadn't been able to give her daughter. 'I say Gladys's voice, but it was my voice that was speaking. It never stopped in my head. You can't imagine how much I talked to myself, how much I spoke to her, Gladys. I asked her why she had chosen me. Did I look like Mother Teresa? I asked her what made her believe that Lisana and I could have been sisters. Was I suicidal? Was I depressed, neurotic, on the verge of killing myself without knowing it?'

She got to know the neighbourhood friends ('kind, attentive, even with Lisana, but from a distance, and deeply affected by the death of their friend'); she got to know Gladys's house ('all the frills, everywhere, it was oppressive'), and she got to know Lisana. 'Not easygoing, not chatty, but after a few days of living together without me asking anything of her, not trying to console her, encourage her, get her to do anything, she understood I would leave her alone. That's all she wanted, to be left to her darkness.'

At the time I knew nothing about Lisana. Her obsession with suicide, her repeated attempts, and Gladys's fight to keep her alive. I learned about it once I was deep in my conversations with Janelle.

The people from whom she was renting a room in the basement got used to seeing me arrive late Friday night and leave late Sunday afternoon. The room was uncomfortable, just one window, tiny, blocked by snow, so there was little light inside and a bathroom that was shared with fellow lodgers. Luckily, Patrice would leave us his house from time to time. He can't stand the invasion of snowmobiles ('It's a nightmare; there are days when it's all you can hear'), and he takes a break from AbeBooks for one week a month to restock his inventory. He goes to one region or another and makes the rounds of library book sales, flea markets, and thrift shops, and he comes back with boxes filled with wonders to unpack.

It was during our first weekend at Patrice's that I learned that he was the internet beau. I saw Janelle's profile lying around with similar profiles in the mountain of papers cluttering up his desk. Janelle spotted what I was looking at but didn't seem bothered. 'Not a reliable lover, your friend; he casts his line all over the place.' Much later, when our affair burned out, I got this explanation from Patrice: 'It keeps me entertained,' he said. 'I write to them for a while, and when it stops entertaining me, I tell them where I live, and poof! They disappear. Janelle was the only one who wasn't afraid of Clova. When I saw that you clicked with her, I let it drop. She did too, by the way. But she wasn't the woman for you either.'

Aside from the snowmobiles, winter in Clova is magnificent. Mainly for the quality of the snow. It is a dazzling white and takes on austere and voluptuous shapes that make it seem like it settles and sculpts itself to the sound of some music directing its movements. But to this powerful white I prefer the hour when the snow awaits the sunset and takes on a cloak of transparent blue. It was during Clova's blue hours that Janelle and I took our most beautiful walks.

She liked Shania Twain, Jill Barber, Mark Knopfler, had no interest in books, none in sports, but would have liked to travel abroad and visit other countries. That was all I knew about her, aside from the fact that she was relieved to get back to her life after having spent over two months in 'a candy store.' She didn't like Gladys's house. She would have left much earlier, but there was Lisana. The funeral was done, the house was going to be put up for sale; a place had to be found for her.

I didn't manage to find out where Lisana was now. Janelle explained in detail the problem of Lisana, who was going to find herself alone with nowhere to live. The neighbourhood friends wanted nothing to do with her ('it was obvious'), Suzan couldn't take her on ('her son is allergic to Lisana'), and the woman in question could not have cared less about what the future held. 'I was the only one left. Gladys had dumped a helluva problem in my lap.'

I have a hard time imagining Janelle in the role of helper. Having moved around a lot, she keeps her distance from sorrows and hassles that don't concern her. She already has a life that she complicates to suit her. And yet, during our conversations – particularly during the blue hours, which are conducive to thought – she would talk about Lisana as if she knew her inside out, as if she had had access to a Lisana that no one else had bothered to get to know, when, according to what Janelle said, they had barely exchanged a few words in Swastika. She had sympathy and even admiration for the woman. 'Her stubbornness, her refusal to let herself sink into the absurdity of days, the strength it took her to resist life's illusions.' And she was outraged. 'What is this tyranny of happiness? Lisana is much better off unhappy than trying to be happy.'

'What did you do with her?'

I could see that Janelle had found in Lisana echoes of her own life. They shared the same hard core, a tight knot, deeply buried, that they protected with all their strength – through inertia in Lisana's case, and through movement and itinerancy in Janelle's.

'Where she is, she has the right to be unhappy. She doesn't bother anyone.'

I wasn't going to learn more. The place where Janelle had put Lisana and her depression would remain off-limits to me. But I knew it existed. Because come the thaw, in March, when all the snowmobiles have is wet snow, it's dead quiet at the Restaurant Clova, and Janelle went away for a week. She came back without telling me where she had been. I didn't insist. I had learned that there was no point forcing open locked doors. Our conversations had to stick to the story of the rail journey that had sparked a romance that – I knew, oh, how I knew – would not survive.

This story was in our bed, in our blue hours, it was the only path that was available to keep me close to her.

I spent the winter going back and forth between Senneterre and Clova.

Did I launch this investigation to fan the nascent flames of the couple we never would become? Not exclusively, because there were also the school trains. It was a marvellous story and the perfect counterpoint to the story of Gladys's journey. I couldn't think of one without thinking of the other. It was the same story when all is said and done. The Gladys who headed out on the rails one fall morning was no different from the one who dreamed of her future to the sound of the clickety-clacks. And I am collecting the pebbles they left behind them.

In the spring of 2013, I made my first trip to Swastika without really knowing what I was searching for or how to go about it. I am an English teacher, not a police investigator, and Frank Smarz's was the only place I could show up, under the pretext of a recent alliance among smokers, but to say what? Ask him what? I was aware of the ridiculousness of my situation.

It is a four-hour drive between Senneterre and Swastika. I had plenty of time to get the measure of my anxiety. I also felt a little drunk. I had never gone to Northern Ontario, and I could feel the tingle of novelty in my body and mind. I was at the beginning of my travels, yet I already considered myself a great traveller.

I had gone through Kirkland Lake, and in leaving town, I spotted on my right a strange structure that criss-crossed the sky with black, disparate shapes. At first I thought it was a scrap-iron dump, but the structure contained lines that were unfamiliar to me, and I made a U-turn. I parked on the road that led to it, and that was when I realized it was a commemorative monument to Kirkland Lake miners. The monument, some ten metres high, was of a mine shaft and five life-size miners frozen in drilling, conveyance, and scaling operations. All in the purest spirit of Soviet realism to the glory of the workers. Three tall black granite headstones listed the names of the miners (three hundred, I counted) who died on the job and the dates of the accidents.

I thought I was at the entrance to a cemetery, but a sign farther along announced it was a museum. And I did what Léonard Mostin did, like lots of travellers with time to kill in Kirkland Lake. I followed the sign and the others marking the winding road, and I met Bernie Jaworsky.

Bernie, I believe I mentioned, is a volunteer at the museum. He had published *Lamps Forever Lit* a few years before, a book that required a great deal of research, I think I also mentioned. And he quickly spotted in me the light-headedness of someone who is standing before the void and hesitating to plunge. 'For me, it was the three hundred names on the monument that led me to the edge of the chasm,' he confided later at the restaurant.

We visited the museum, which I liked less and less as I discovered its reason for being. A museum devoted to Harry Oakes (the museum had been his home), a magnate of the mines where the men on the monument died and who was mysteriously assassinated in his luxurious home in the Bahamas. I didn't understand how you could celebrate both the miners and the person who let them die on the job. Obviously, I said none of this. Bernie was eager, affable, attentive, and cared about showing me the museum. But what was crying out inside me did not escape him once we were in front of the museum centrepiece, Nancy's Room, the bedroom of the Oakes's eldest girl, with its plaster ornaments. I didn't ooh and aah in wonder as expected, offered not even a nod of appreciation. The birds, the animals, all the nice stories, Don Quixote, Humpty Dumpty, engraved in the plaster on the walls for the pleasure of the darling little girl of a killer in the mines only amplified my grumbling.

At the restaurant, I vented my feelings. Bernie listened to me dispassionately without interrupting, and when I had said all I had to say, when I had worked through my shock and there was nothing left for me to do but eat my pierogies, Bernie looked at me with all the attention of his small, searching eyes and said: 'There is no contradiction. If there's something we respect here, it's work and money.'

My revolt, my noble feelings, were a familiar discourse to him. 'There are families who lost someone to Harry Oakes's mine and refuse to set foot in the museum.' He had let me give free rein to my emotions, and he waited until they served the coffee to ask me what brought me to this part of the world.

He didn't know anything about the school trains, but he was familiar with Gladys's story. 'Everyone here knows it, but what you are looking for is going to take you much further than you think. You won't come through it unscathed.'

He was right, he is always right, my friend Bernie. I got lost in lands that drove me ever further without getting the final word on the story. I went off in search of the school trains, of everything about Gladys, and myself, it seems, because the man who was coming and going to meet strangers discovered another way of being in the world. I would come home, to my habits, to everything that had always seemed too small and that now seemed to have new dimensions. I was at home, I was listening to the radio, I was buying groceries, I was jogging, but I was also in Chapleau, Swastika, Metagama, Sudbury. I was at the centre of a constellation of people I had met all over, some of whom had become friends, whom I found in my notes, on my iPhone, and who accompanied me wherever I went. I was obsessed. My thoughts were restless, there were conversations, back and forth, and when the chatter got too loud, when it started contradicting itself, I would head off to check what everyone had said.

Weekends, Christmas holidays, Easter, and the summer break (blessed be the occupation of teacher), I spent them all on the road, on trains, always moving and now chained to my computer. I wonder whether there will be an end to all this.

I lost Janelle along the way. It was written in the stars. There was no way she was going to change the course of her life for me. She needs movement, excitement; a humble English teacher from a sleepy little town is not going to keep her on her toes. All I hoped was that it would last a little longer. We made it a little more than a year in a sort of suspension of time, with me going almost every weekend to Clova and her astonished to see me arrive, as if our story were starting over each time.

She was the one who had the idea for a trip to Paris. I never would have dared suggest it. It was an outlandish, fabulous, irresistible idea.

'What if we went to see him in Paris, your Léonard Mostin?'

I don't know whether it was the desire for travel, whether Clova was starting to get her down, or whether she really believed it when she said that the key to the mystery of Gladys would be found in Paris. 'Your Léonard Mostin, he was at the station that morning; he was waiting for the train with Gladys. He may know something no one else does. You have no idea the sorts of things that are said between travellers when they are waiting. Two strangers who are going to part and forget one another talk to the other as if talking to themselves. Who knows what Gladys told him that morning?'

We were those two strangers, Janelle and me, in the bed where we explored each other without her ever giving me the key to her mystery. I didn't know what held her in this state of want, continuously in movement, always about to leave, and she never asked me about my life in Senneterre, past loves, or anything else. She was solidly in the present, waiting for a more promising place to give her a sign. I was afraid of the moment I would lose her, and I said yes to Paris. I secretly hoped that, during the short time we would be a couple on a trip, she would reveal herself to me.

I had collected all the information to recreate Gladys's itinerary, and I had come to her motivation, what had driven her to the rails, and, what obsessed me even more, what intrigued me even more, was what she had said to her daughter that morning of September 24 that could have made Lisana believe there was a suicide pact. A supposed pact because no one, not Suzan, not Janelle, not Frank Smarz, no one believed such a horrible thing. But something had to have been said that morning to convince the daughter to let her mother go and that could enlighten us as to Gladys's motivations. All that remained was that glimpse of possibility, a conversation with a stranger the morning of her departure, Léonard Mostin.

It was Desmond, Suzan's son, who put us on the scent of the man people thought to be a Jewish historian. The handyman poet had become a novelist and had unexpected success with his first book, a historical novel about the Ojibwe massacre at Frederick House, which earned him many awards and invitations around the world. He ended up at a literary festival in France, and it was there, in Vincennes, at the Festival America, that he met Léonard Mostin.

I should have known when Janelle arrived with everything she owned. 'Ready for the big adventure,' she said to me, pushing two huge garbage bags in front of her. And this was in addition to the enormous knapsack that was digging into her back. It all weighed at least one hundred kilos. Neither of us had travelled by plane, but I knew they wouldn't take it. 'They won't take it? Oh well, I'll leave some here.' Elation! She had quit her job to go on a trip with me, and she was leaving me three quarters of her possessions. 'I'll pick it up when we come back.' I believed her. I'll admit that I thought there was a chance for her and me, when we came back, in my bungalow, my little town. It was ridiculous. She was ready for somewhere much more interesting than here.

She is an impressive woman. It was the first trip to Europe for both of us, and I was astonished by her facility for finding her way on the RER, the metro, everywhere really, and the strange language she started to speak, a sort of Parisian Québécois, with Franco-Ontarian tones ('absolutely delicious,' Léonard Mostin said, under her spell). All her senses were on alert. We would leave in the morning from Rue Serpente (a small old-fashioned hotel, room the size of a thimble), and we wouldn't have taken more than two strides before I would feel her rise up above the sidewalk in a state of receptivity to everything that was on offer. She had already left me.

What can I say about Léonard Mostin? He is an intellectual, a lover of books – his tiny apartment was full of them, they spilled over everywhere – and he was delighted to play host to us, we who had come from the wide-open spaces that filled his novel. He was likeable, attentive to our questions, and, above all, curious about us, our life *over there* in what he called 'the land of the dark comedians.'

The conversation we had hoped for hadn't taken place; he and Gladys hadn't even exchanged words, but he was generous. He described her as he had seen her that morning. Hair white like snow, cut square, the three-quarter-length coat or rather a thick puffy jacket that fell to mid-thigh, and the tote bag that was her only luggage. An old woman, he said, leaning against the station wall, not moving, not seeing, who was waiting for the train without really waiting for it. 'What was she really waiting for? For the train to go by and leave her there waiting? Or had she already left? Somewhere else, far away from herself, maybe she was overwhelmed, devastated, overcome by what lay ahead of her. I started to approach her, and I realized that the woman was carrying death inside her.'

The words! The words and such conviction; I felt like I was wandering in the middle of a novel. I let him say it. But Janelle pounced immediately.

'Why … What makes you think that? … '

'Her smell.'

' … Her smell?'

'She smelled like my mother when she was dying. It's not something you forget.'

I felt another novelesque flight in the making, which he held back because Janelle wasn't going to let the first one go.

'A smell … of wax?'

'Exactly. A waxy smell. How did you know?'

'That was the smell coming out of Gladys's bed. But when I met her, during all those days on the trains, she didn't smell like that. Do you have extrasensory perception or something?' (He shook his head.) 'When I think about her, that's the smell that comes back to me, and I like it. I can bring it back whenever I want by doing this.' (She touched her fingertips together and placed them under her nose like one does for an object when you want to be sure of the smell.) 'That was your mother's smell?'

Was that when I lost her? When they were sitting across from each other at the tiny table in Léonard Mostin's tiny apartment, sniffing the flesh of their fingers and looking at each other as if they shared a secret?

We spent ten days in Paris, and Léonard Mostin was with us for all ten of them. He took us to the Champs-Élysées, Notre-Dame, Père-Lachaise cemetery, Sacré-Coeur, all of which he called 'the Paris of tourists,' and he took us to his Paris, with its narrow winding streets that change names at every turn, the squares (the Franco-Ontarian was astonished to learn the English word was used), the little terraced bistros ('You sit facing the street?'), and I could see him amused at our astonishment. I wondered whether we were going to become characters in his novel. Along with the swearing Ukrainian from the cemetery and the young Indigenous lover, he talked about them as if he had met them the day before and had had long conversations with them. If Gladys had become an old woman who carried death within her, what would become of us? I could see us wandering in the streets of his novel, unrefined but endearing characters, me a bit humdrum and Janelle who went charging ahead of herself and transformed before your very eyes. I understood pretty quickly who the novelist's focus was on.

At the Musée d'Orsay, in front of a painting by van Gogh, I had a revelation of what would be our undoing. Janelle was in front of the self-portrait of van Gogh. Janelle was no longer Janelle.

Do I need to spell out that I'm not an art lover?

I had let them leave me behind in the rooms of the museum. I was tired of standing in front of paintings and waiting for their comments. To my great surprise, Janelle had as much to say as Léonard Mostin. When I caught up with them, they were in front of the painting by van Gogh, both of them speechless, Janelle completely transformed, her features brought together in a point that illuminated her face, her eyes with the same steady stare as those of van Gogh. She was no longer her own, she was the gaze that was gazing at her. And beside her, Léonard Mostin was wonderstruck.

Did I really see the tear on her cheek, or was it pure imagination on my part? She was in such a state of excitement, at once pain and rapture, that I could believe anything.

'I never thought I would see this painting in real life,' she said, turning to Léonard Mostin.

He asked her whether it was her favourite van Gogh. She told him that the nights churning with colour were what was most beautiful about van Gogh, and she asked him whether she could see *Café Terrace at Night.* 'Not here,' Léonard Mostin said. Probably in Amsterdam. That's where the largest van Gogh museum is.' And from one thing to another, always about how dazzling van Gogh's colours were and the artist's great humanity, she said this sentence that lifted the veil of the mystery of Janelle.

She said: 'Van Gogh is what did me in.'

It was more than was needed to pique the novelist's curiosity. And there, at the Musée d'Orsay, before van Gogh's self-portrait, we heard her whole history. Studies at the School of Fine Arts, years throwing colours on canvas that refused to take life, the conviction that she was worthless, that she would always be worthless, that van Gogh was the one who found the way of colour, that there would never be any other, particularly not her. 'I learned to live without illusions,' she said. 'I thought it was over, that I was bulletproof, that I would never have another artistic emotion.'

I wasn't surprised when she announced that she would not be going home with me. Too many signs had piled up during our final days in Paris. Léonard Mostin, who would never leave us alone, the discussions I felt excluded from; I was nothing more than a little pet dog sniffing around the bone I was thrown during the conversation.

There were no heartrending goodbyes. One last night, a mid-air kiss when I boarded the RER for the airport, and it was done. Nice and clean.

It was a month before I got an email. She had visited the museums of Amsterdam and Otterlo, with Léonard obviously ('he's super'), he had taken her to visit Vincent's and Theo's graves at Auvers-sur-Oise, she had seen the room at the inn where the artist died and 'You'll never guess. I saw the wheat field with crows, the real one, not the painting, the field where Vincent van Gogh set up his easel to make his painting.'

That was all I would get from her. An email here and there that talked about this and that, when all that mattered to me was what it didn't say and what I felt behind every word. Léonard Mostin had had access to that part of her I was excluded from. They had become intimate. I can feel it in the *we* that gets away from her sometimes, which she never said about the two of us. I did not measure up to the novelist, I'll admit. He succeeded where I failed.

'Anyway, she wasn't the woman for you.'

That's what Bernie told me when I returned from Paris and what he repeats every time I bring up Janelle. My romantic defeat doesn't interest him. It's Léonard Mostin the novelist who has all of his attention. Léonard Mostin, who, across the ocean, in his mouse hole (he really likes *mouse hole*; it's miserable, pathetic, squalid, joyful), amuses himself rewriting lives.

'A man who can turn Gladys into an old woman who carries death inside her is capable of anything.'

I can see that he is afraid for himself, for his neighbours and friends, the people of Kirkland Lake and Swastika whom the novelist met during his great adventure on Canadian soil and who for the time being are only imaginary creatures, figments of a fanciful mind, but as soon as they touch paper, it will be a nightmare.

'I don't want to wake up one morning and see myself as a *lumbering man weighed down by regret* or in a sort of *transience of a cunning mind* as it pleases the gentleman to imagine me in his novel.'

He is waiting for 'the real story' that will reassert the facts, 'nothing but the facts, don't go thinking you're a novelist,' and that has been so long in coming. I thought I could never do it. The cursor blinked for so long on my screen without me adding the word it was waiting for. And then, one day, shortly after my return from Paris, I went back to my computer and, to my great astonishment, the words came thick and fast on the screen. Like torpedoes, as if I were at war, as if I were liberating myself. Pages streamed by, pages spoke out, pages called to me. Sometimes I would get up in the middle of the night to shut them up. I would pick up where I had left off; I finished the sentence that had dragged me out of bed, and I would find myself with something else calling out to me. The sun would rise, and I would still be in front of my screen.

I wrote in this frenetic state until Janelle appeared in the story and everything got muddled. I kept Bernie's instructions in mind. But how to stick to the facts when every word, every sentence, whipped up a smell, a movement of the head, a shift of her gaze that made me dizzy? The story was moving along painfully. The pages were stifled, the pages were swallowing me up. I spent months struggling in a story that wouldn't advance. Until, looking for I don't know what in a cupboard in the basement, I found the garbage bags. A wave of emotion swept over me. All of Janelle's things were there, in these bags, which I hadn't opened. I could see her, hear her, feel her through the polyethylene of the bags. Which I absolutely must not open, I knew. Janelle would come out of them like a genie from a bottle and would haunt my mind forever. And I did what I should have done long ago. I shipped the bags to Marie-Luce on the next train.

A good decision. The story resumed its steady pace, but it could not ignore Janelle. She was and will remain intimately tied to the story and my life.

I don't know when I will be done with this chronicle. Just when I think I have written everything there is to know, someone catches my attention. When it isn't Gladys, it's Lisana and her supposed madness (I have no strong opinion on the matter), or Frank Smarz, who remains guilty of dark intentions. Even now, there is always someone shoving my nose in my mess. Or a new fact that I become aware of. Or a contradiction, an inconsistency, suddenly appears. And I have to phone, email, get back on the road. My cursor can wait for days, sometimes weeks, before I get back to it. Not to mention, obviously, my work at the high school that demands its due.

Bernie often asks me how it's going. I tell him that the pages are piling up, but I can't picture the day when I will see the last word. Léonard Mostin will have published his novel well before I have finished with my chronicle.

'Don't worry' (and an impish smile appears). 'He has that wild-eyed woman, and she will ruin his novel.'

I received emails from Janelle for a while. She pursued her passion for van Gogh. After the museums in Amsterdam and Otterlo, she visited those in Prague and Zurich and was planning to go to London to see the famous *Self-Portrait with Bandaged Ear*. With Léonard, obviously, still just as 'super.'

I entertained no illusions. Janelle had flown off again. She had rediscovered herself and was spreading her wings wide. Léonard Mostin had become her guide and companion. The two of them lived in their own inner worlds, but they had found the fast track to romantic intimacy in artistic emotion. There was nothing I could do about a track that was inaccessible to me.

But I continued our correspondence, if only to reassure Bernie, who would come regularly for news. They had just returned from Munich, they were going to Prague, they were thinking of going to London, and every time it was good news because Janelle was keeping the author from his novel.

For a while I got bogged down. During this time when I was half-heartedly pursuing my investigation, I would go to Bernie's from time to time. I would see him search for the spark in my eyes, the spark of someone who is on a quest, but it was no longer there. I came and went because I was carrying inside me a life that wasn't my own – Gladys, Lisana, and all the others – and I had the feeling that, if I stopped coming and going with them in mind, my own life would vanish. It would have lost its meaning.

Suzan was in a bit of the same state. I hadn't returned to Metagama, but I would call her when the weather was good and satellite communication permitted. I imagined her in her little house: the phone rings, she jumps, who could be calling her, she could pick up now but lets it ring, approaches the phone that is vibrating at the end of the kitchen counter, and with the sudden strike of an animal, she picks up the handset and asks: 'Who's calling?' I've always been surprised by her habit of snapping at you. Normally it was after the fourth ring that I would hear her hoarse voice, sticky with phlegm. She wouldn't have spoken for days.

Now she answered on the first ring with such a worried 'Hello?' that I could almost hear what she wasn't saying: 'Desmond? Is that you?' Desmond was in New York, Toronto, London, carried off in a whirlwind of success. He managed to extricate himself from the whirlwind from time to time, and he would show up with groceries that could keep her for a month. But for all the rest, firewood, things that needed repair, she didn't know how she was going to manage. On the phone she told me: 'I thought he was the one who needed me.' Her voice trailed off, sounded old.

The voice grew weaker over the months. She was delighted with her son's success, but she could see that he didn't have time to devote to her anymore. 'He arrives and leaves on the same gust of wind.' She was starting to think she would need to leave the house, her trees, the whistle of the trains, the clickety-clacks, all the things that had kept her company through the years. But to go where, that she didn't know. 'I don't want to be a little old lady in a condo. I don't want to spend my days looking at the wall across the way.' She had started to pack her boxes.

I got an email from Janelle, longer than normal, because she couldn't stop marvelling at what she had seen in London. Monet, Gauguin, Cézanne, van Gogh obviously, and his famous *Self-Portrait with Bandaged Ear*. 'The colours are powerful. How could a man so dark make colour vibrate that way?' Other equally enthusiastic comments followed about what she had seen and admired in London, and then, at the very end, as a postscript, as if she were giving it to me in passing, Lisana's address in Toronto. I knew it was the last email, that there would be no more. She was leaving Lisana in my hands so she could fly away to a new life.

The spark came back, I was once again coming and going in search of something that awaited me, something that would shed light on the path behind me without knowing where it would take me next.

Lisana, it was obviously Lisana, that was lighting the new terrain.

If Janelle had left me Lisana's address, it meant that she was alive, that she hadn't given in to her suicidal impulse. I'm no psychologist, no psychiatrist, nothing that gives me any authority, but nevertheless, a question was nagging at me. How do you live when you have given up on the desire to die? I remember what Bernie had said to me. *There is a sense of power in playing with your life*. What had she found that convinced her to give up that powerful drive?

For the few more years than my investigation required, I would go fairly regularly to Toronto. (The address will remain confidential in case there are readers of this story. I don't want people to go bothering Lisana in her non-existence. Which, I must say, she is not doing too badly at.)

I was cautious in my initial approaches. I kept in mind everything I had been told about her and everything I had thought when I saw her at the restaurant in Clova. Did she see me then? Was she even aware of my presence? Probably not. I was a total stranger, and I had to use tact so that she wouldn't dig in her heels or just flat-out take off when I approached.

The building I found myself in front of was a women's shelter. A man couldn't hang around there without the police being called. Luckily, there were things to keep me busy, or at least keep me looking busy, around the shelter.

The building was colourful. It didn't have the discreet look of a place where battered women could find shelter and protection. It looked more like a big candy tied in ribbon that awaited the little kids at the corner of a street. Caramel colour, the windows a nice creamy white, and its walls featured long strips of pink, lemon yellow, and pistachio green, and on these strips were words that invited hope and reconciliation. That is what I understood from what I could read in French and English. Most of it was in languages and alphabets that were foreign to me.

The immediate surroundings were just as colourful. It was a long line of container restaurants that served modest cuisine, of different origins, particularly Asian, to a clientele that was just as diverse. Sometimes I was the only white man going container to container, with an eye on the women's building.

It took several hours of stuffing myself with ceviche, mango lassis, and I don't know what else before I saw Lisana leave the building. Without hair hanging down her back and without her headphones on, my first surprise. She came out at the same time as a young Indigenous woman with whom she exchanged a few words – second surprise – and without hesitation, she headed right. She walked quickly, with a determined step. She turned left on a street where the currents of a lively crowd intersected. I headed off after her.

I walked behind her, taking care to leave just the right number of people between us so as not to alert her or lose her from sight. The crowd grew thicker; people were heading home from work. I had a hard time keeping up the pace and the distance, but a few heads away I saw Lisana's, straight and imposing, which was staying its course. She didn't look left or right; she looked at nothing, in fact, not even the traffic lights when she stopped at a street corner. I walked for a long time, a very long time. I no longer knew where I was. I had eyes only for the head straight like an arrow in the fray. There was a moment when the crowd parted as young teens went by on rollerblades, then it reformed, and I found myself right behind her. I wondered whether the moment had come to show myself.

At the red light that awaited us at the corner of a street, I slipped up to her left and turned toward her, but the light had already changed, and she had resumed walking with her confident step. We walked for a long time like two robots, looking straight ahead, steps synchronized, almost military, and nothing to suggest that she was uncomfortable with, intrigued by, or even aware of my presence, while I was in the midst of working out a greeting to introduce myself to her.

An ambulance went by. Flashing lights and deafening siren. I looked toward the street, then Lisana, and I didn't take my eyes off her after that. And her, still nothing, as if I weren't there. I was able to scrutinize her at leisure. It was the Lisana I had met in Clova, locked deep inside herself, but with a different energy, looking younger with a haircut that showed off her neck. The headphones were there, around her neck, in case of need, if the ambient sound wasn't enough. That's what I understood later during our long walks, because it never failed; we walked the city in every direction every time I visited, and I would see her put her headphones on when, for example, we would head into a residential area, an area that was too calm for her liking.

Hours passed and the day grew darker. We were now striding along almost deserted sidewalks; were we going to walk to the end of the night? She had no itinerary. I could tell by her way of taking one street and then another, left, right, left, a trajectory that was often circular, that had no other purpose than walking, walking, walking, and clearing her head — that too I understood.

I tapped her on the shoulder. I don't know how the gesture came to me, but that's what I did, tap her on the shoulder like you would knock on a door to announce your presence at a friend's or a stranger's, and she opened it. She looked at me, really looked at me, and I saw the bewilderment, the confusion, the simmering of her thoughts, I saw intense brain activity in her eyes and, after a moment that seemed to me like an eternity, I heard her say to me in a tone that reflected her pride and relief at having figured it out: 'You're Janelle's friend.'

She had been expecting me; I had been announced. In the flash of an instant she must have seen the surprise and bewilderment in my eyes, probably also a bit of euphoria, because I had an image of Janelle holding out an invisible hand to us and smiling at us from the distant place where she was. A crooked smile; Janelle never smiles outright.

'She sent me a postcard,' Lisana told me, and what followed was the detailed, confused story of postcards she'd received from Paris, London, Amsterdam, pretty much everywhere in Europe. She talked to me while we continued our walk. It would always be that way. We roam the city. She talks, she talks, always looking straight ahead, never slowing the pace, not a concern for me. Sometimes it is confused and mixed up; sometimes it is clear and unclouded. I will never know whether the real Lisana is found in the confusion or the clarity of expression. Or she plows ahead without a word for hours, and I have to pick up the pace to follow her. Her brain works at the same rhythm as her legs, a dynamo that never stops.

She works at the women's shelter. That's what she told me at our first meeting. She does a bit of everything, cleaning and cooking, in exchange for a salary that is just enough to pay for the room Janelle found her in one of the row houses that border a highway. For the reason previously mentioned, I will not reveal the name of the street where Lisana has her room. She is at her best there, I think. At least a ten-kilometre walk to get there, an impersonal, anonymous residential area, the horrible noise of the highway, all things that contributed to the room's charm and affordability.

We went our separate ways without a goodbye (she turned her back to me, and I did likewise), and thank god for my iPhone because my feet were on fire, and I could call a taxi to get back to my hotel. The next day, I went shopping for some running shoes, and I showed up at the shelter at the end of the day. She showed no surprise, joy, or displeasure. We walked.

People often ask about Lisana, what became of her, how she remembered her mother, whether she was happy or unhappy in her new life. Lisana, happy? There is no point even asking. I think she has managed not to be and has found in this non-existence shelter from life's demands. She couldn't care less about being happy or unhappy, living or dying. From her suicidal obsession she has kept only the obsession. An obsession with no focus that compels her to roam the city in search of nothing. She lives in a void, and it suits her perfectly.

And Gladys, does Lisana talk about her mother? The question comes mainly from Suzan. The answer is difficult because Gladys fell into the large void like all the rest, and she comes out only when I say her name. I am waiting for a story to escape from her when sometimes a knot undoes in her brain and I ask, regardless of whether Lisana is telling me about a new resident arriving at the shelter or an incident in the kitchen: 'And Gladys, what did she do?' as if her mother were part of the story. 'Mom?… ' I can feel her searching. 'Mooommmm?' The word is drawn out, the o's have more space between them, expand, transform. 'Moooommmm,' I can almost see her smile at herself and finally, 'Moooommm would never have messed up the meringue,' or something else that honours her mother, the best cook in the world, the most marvellous of women.

She hasn't forgotten anything, it's all there, but deeply buried, and it takes her a few seconds of sifting through her brain for the memory to emerge.

Janelle, on the other hand, is never far away. She is present in her mind. Probably because of the postcards. There is no need to activate the brain. She talks about her with ease as we criss-cross the city. Just as she talks to me about the shelter residents. They are part of a present that is hers but not entirely, a present she experiences from a distance. I am always surprised to see her talk with the few women who are getting some fresh air at the door of the building. They are nomadic, unstable, mistreated, abused women. They smoke, joke, laugh, cry, console each other. Sorrow turns golden in the sun on the sidewalk. Lisana crosses through the laughter and the tears, returns greetings, adds what is called for, and heads off with her robotic step. She is at peace with her environment.

If I still felt I had the right to communicate with Janelle, I would congratulate her because I think the women's shelter is the perfect place for Lisana. *Where she is, she has the right to be unhappy. She doesn't bother anyone.* It took me seeing Lisana cross through the group of women on the sidewalk to understand Janelle's words. There was no dissonance, no unease. Lisana is comfortable in the sorrow of others.

I would also congratulate Gladys. Obviously, that's impossible, and I don't think she would appreciate it. She wanted light, gentleness, everything honey for her daughter's life. She wouldn't appreciate her spending her time with a mound of pain. But I would congratulate her. For having instinctively known that Janelle was the person Lisana needed.

I think that now I am part of her world, and that if she occasionally chats with someone at the shelter I must come up in conversation as a relative or distant friend who visits her from time to time. Sometimes I try to imagine what she says about that friend. A guy in a baseball cap who always has a gift for her and who doesn't bug her too much, even though he is fast on her heels when he comes to Toronto. A casual friend, not too much trouble, rather pleasant company.

When I get back from Toronto, people ask whether she talked about Gladys and – because the question still haunts us – whether she let anything slip about the fateful morning of September 24.

I have precious little to report. Lisana lives – exists – in a present that is running on empty and at high speed. Our conversations happen in fits and starts, kilometres of silence apart. And they are often mundane. The menu at the shelter, the potatoes she hates peeling, AC/DC, Kiss, Metallica, her favourite music, until I slip in the name of her mother, and Gladys appears in her mind. It's also quite mundane. A dress that her mother made her, a canary-yellow dress, a dress that she didn't like ('too girly') but that she wore bravely to Sunday service. Her mother's pride as she showed off her report cards ('I had all A's'). The figurine ('a ballerina in a cotton-candy-pink tutu') that she broke while jumping rope a little too close to it and that Gladys spent hours gluing back together. It's affectionate and respectful, and it's always praising her mother, the most wonderful of women.

I'm not trying to stir up bitter memories, no direct questions or stealthy interrogation; I don't want to startle her. But I had to address the morning of September 24 in some way or another. And it was when a particularly affectionate 'Mooomm' slipped into the conversation that the opportunity arose. We were talking about trips she would take with her mother on the train.

'You didn't try to go with her the morning she left?'

We were at the corner of Yonge and Queen, a particularly noisy area. I was afraid my question would get lost in the bustle of the crowd.

'No, she told me to wait.'

'She asked you to wait for her?'

'No, she told me to wait. She said she would send someone to me.'

I was stunned. I had never gotten so much information. I wanted to keep going with it, but people were rushing around us. It was the end of the workday. We were in front of the Eaton Centre at the heart of the shopping frenzy. There was a terrible racket. There was no way to have a sustained conversation.

We continued along Yonge Street, me lagging a little behind and above all supremely disappointed at having let go of a promising conversation. North of College Street, however, there was a slight lull in the decibels and that was when, without a preamble, and without slowing her pace, Lisana turned to me and said: 'Mom was wrong. I got a brother, not a sister.'

That was in March, during the long school holiday. I can't make the trip to Toronto unless I have a few days ahead of me. Despite the nine hours of driving, I like leaving winter, which lingers where I live, to find myself in near spring. At the beginning of March in Toronto, the cherry trees aren't yet in flower, the grass isn't green, and nothing is budding or chirping, but you can smell spring in the air.

I regretfully left the mildness of Toronto for the long trip home with the intention of stopping at my friend Bernie's in Kirkland Lake. I needed his advice.

As usual, Bernie let me get it all off my chest without interrupting. I could recite to him, almost word for word, the conversation Lisana and I had on Yonge Street and her completely unanticipated way of declaring her friendship. 'Her brother,' I said to him. 'Can you imagine? That's what I have become to her.'

Bernie had a completely different interpretation.

'It's the tail of the comet, the missing piece of the puzzle.'

There was a twinkle in his eye. I didn't understand what he was saying. It was only after he told me a long story that I could follow his line of thought.

'Gladys was looking for the pharaoh's daughter.'

I hesitate a bit here before unravelling the whole story, because it is ridiculous, outlandish, absolutely incredible, and yet it is the only one that holds water. We all ended up believing it – well, almost all of us.

'Gladys took to the rails in an impulse of desperate hope.'

The story is biblical. It goes back to the beginning of time. The Book of Exodus, chapter two. It is the story of baby Moses, placed by his mother in a basket on the waters of the Nile. It was the only way his mother could find to save her child from persecution by the pharaoh, who had ordered all male Israelite newborns to be put to death. The hoped-for miracle arrived in the person of the pharaoh's daughter. It was the hour of her daily ablutions in the Nile, and she heard the infant's cries. She ordered her servant to go fetch the basket from which the cries emerged. Charmed by the child's beauty, she decided to adopt him. She asked her servant to go in search of a wet nurse. It so happened that the servant was baby Moses's sister. You can imagine who the servant turned to. That was how the baby Moses came to be nursed by his birth mother. Raised in the pharaoh's court, once grown up, little Moses discovered his Jewish origins and was handed by God (the episode of the burning bush) the mission to free his people from slavery and lead them to the Promised Land.

'It takes mad hope to entrust the fate of your child to the river.'

Bernie believes that Gladys was trying to save her daughter beyond her own death and that, just like baby Moses's mother, she took a huge gamble. She set out on the rails hoping to meet someone, somewhere, to whom she could entrust her suicidal daughter.

'Janelle wasn't picked at random; she was where Gladys was waiting for her.'

This story is at the limit of common sense and contrary to everything I know about Bernie. A measured, thoughtful man, loyal husband, responsible father, he is good sense incarnate. How did he come up with such a nonsensical story?

'It wasn't a question of common sense for Gladys, any more than for the mother of baby Moses. Extreme situations call for extreme solutions.'

I resisted, I made every possible argument against it. Gladys was too clear-headed, too reasonable to set out on a quest for a pharaoh's daughter. Lisana was too dependent on her mother to let her leave. Solid arguments, I thought. But there was nothing for it, Bernie kept his calm and his smile. My old friend had arrived at the end of reflections he had been harbouring for a long time, and at the end of this long tunnel he found 'the missing piece,' the key to the riddle, what had motivated Gladys's journey along the Northern rails.

'Let things fall into place. Give yourself time, and at some point, it will become as plain as day to you. That woman was born on the sunny side of life; she could cling to a twig, to anything, to stay on the side of hope, light, beauty, happiness. She couldn't leave this life without having found an emergency exit for her daughter.'

There was plenty of resistance when I in turn told the story of the pharaoh's daughter. First, I had to convince myself that I believe it, and not by half measures, to risk presenting such an unbelievable story. It's delusional, outlandish, inane, and, for some, monstrous. But it's all we have, the only explanation that stands up, the only possible logic to an impossible story. What should we believe if not that Gladys set out to find a pharaoh's daughter for her daughter?

There are different ways to refute this interpretation of Gladys's travels. The most savage and predictable came from Frank Smarz. He took the biblical story apart piece by piece, like he would have a lawn-mower motor, to demonstrate that the two stories don't match. The waters of the Nile, baby Moses's mother, the pharaoh's daughter versus the Northern trains, Lisana's mother, Janelle (or me). A lawn mower and a vacuum cleaner. The pieces don't fit. 'Who is in the wicker basket, who is on the train? The mother of the child to be saved or baby Moses? Gladys or Lisana? For your stories to work together, it would have to be Lisana on the train.'

He is pretty proud of his argument, and he is going to stand by it. The last time I went to Swastika, he was busy with his dandelion wine, and he said to me, as if I had come back again to test my biblical interpretation: 'So are you the brother, the sister, or the servant?' I let it go, and I left him to his smelly vats. No good would come of his wine, but he was going to stand by that too.

Suzan still holds a grudge against him. She has not forgotten the silence and the vacant windows that greeted her when she arrived from Swastika with Desmond. Deadly passivity, recklessness, or pure foolishness? Suzan leaves the question unanswered, but that doesn't stop her from weighing the heft of her grudge in her hands. As for me, I got nothing out of the neighbourhood friends that would shed any light on their intentions. (Sorry, Bernie my friend, the question will not find an answer in the pages that follow. I have come to the end of the story, at least I think so, and I hope I will have the wisdom not to start running after all the remaining questions.)

Suzan hasn't forgotten, 'but since Lisana is alive … ' she is giving Frank Smarz the benefit of the doubt. 'That man believes only in what he sees, and he has blinders as big as sections of wall. He sees virtually nothing, and he's perfectly happy with that.'

She is generally more relaxed, less quick to anger. I visit her regularly since she moved to Clova. We found her a little house that was not too rundown, and we fixed it up. Patrice and me. Desmond came to lend a hand from time to time. The house is the same dark red as the Restaurant Clova, and like the restaurant it has a porch with an awning. Weather permitting, Suzan sits in her rocking chair on the porch watching the trains go by. Because of course the house is a few feet from the tracks. She vibrates just as much as she did in Metagama when the trains go by, the din just as pleasant to Suzan's ears, but no clickety-clack.

No clickety-clack, but the satisfaction of having escaped condo life and having rebuilt her solitude in the middle of nowhere.

Surprisingly, it wasn't so much the solitary life or the house near the tracks that won her over, but the most beautiful cemetery in the world. 'That's where I want to be buried. All that greenery overlooking the lake, it's the most beautiful cemetery you could ever wish for. And I'll still be able to hear the trains from there.'

She is no longer a forest hermit or even a semi-hermit. There are days when people are swarming around her. For example, on Sundays when the Transcontinental arrives and she goes to get her groceries for the week. Patrice takes care of transferring her boxes to the back of the Nath Express. He also does small repairs for her. And for bigger jobs, for example, stacking firewood for the winter, the two of us pitch in, or the three of us when Desmond manages to tear himself away from the literati. After seeing to the wood, we eat the supper that Suzan has prepared and that goes on late into the night, because we all have a lot to say. Desmond, who is travelling the world with his novel; Patrice, who is also travelling the world but via the internet; and I, who continues to come and go between Swastika, Toronto, Senneterre, and Clova. Suzan is the only one who isn't on the move. She is the gravitational core of our little community, 'her boys,' as she calls us.

She eventually got behind the story of the pharaoh's daughter. At first she didn't like it. Because a train isn't a wisp of straw that you randomly entrust with your luck, because Gladys is not an adventurer, because she would have left her old friend from way back at least a branch to hang on to to understand something about the whole story. I think it's the idea that Gladys had excluded her from her rescue plan that she finds intolerable. And then, talking about it around the table with her boys, she came to the conclusion that the story is befitting of Gladys, befitting of her incredible instinct for life.

'Gladys was right all along. Lisana is alive, she has found some balance, and she has someone to watch over her.'

Sometimes I wonder whether Gladys isn't with us, with her incredible optimism, because around the table there is such a desire to find a comforting explanation.

Desmond is the one who lays the groundwork for the conversation, the one who is searching for meaning, and, with the help of some wine, he can have flights of fancy that leave us perplexed and admiring.

'Gladys is a great woman. She outwitted destiny. She is protecting her daughter from beyond the grave. The heroes of this world aren't who you think.'

The poet has become a novelist, and he won't let this story become mere anecdote. Every time Desmond joins us, we know there will be lyricism and metaphor at the table. The wine will flow freely (I now know that Suzan prefers red), and we will be there late into the night, rewriting the stories that fall into our hands. Suzan doesn't last until the end of our evenings. She resists as long as she can, her head bobbing, dozing in fits and starts and coming back to us, rambling for a moment in the conversation, and gradually we see her sink down into her chair. Desmond, with the utmost precaution, almost without waking her, guides her to her bedroom. How many times before the grim reaper takes her from us? We will all be orphans.

As for me, I've accepted the confusion and haze. There is too much to lose trying to explain everything. I am no longer trying to scale high walls that rise up in front of me. The essential truth is found in the cracks, and I am not going to slip into them. I have already dug too much, gotten too tied up in knots that can't be undone. All the pages behind me weigh on me. And I have never bothered to print them. Paper would lend them a reality that I wouldn't be able to avoid. Because all these pages wait. They are full, bouncing, quivering, and they are asking me to spring them from their bytes. But what will I do with them once they are printed? No one has read them, not even I who doesn't remember what the first one contains, and around me there will be pressure to do something with them.

'You're wrong. You'll feel liberated. The weight of the pages will be lifted once they are printed.'

'How will VIA Rail know that an old woman died because they got rid of the train that would take her home if you don't send them your report?'

'What do you think they will do at VIA Rail when they receive a thick wad of paper in the mail? They're going to toss it in the garbage.'

'And no one will have read it. You'll have written all that for nothing.'

'You have to publish it. The only way to release yourself from the story is to publish it.'

'I'm not a writer.'

'You don't need to be a writer to be an author.'

'I could never have my name on the cover of a book.'

'Ask Desmond. He'll claim authorship without a second thought.'

'If it were me, I would let the story wander on the trains. That's where it should be. Train to train. Like Gladys, like the baby Moses, and it will always find a traveller who will read it, and then another, and then another. If you let it wander on the trains, your story will live forever.'

No one has read it, but everyone has something to say about it. It has become shared property. I don't really feel dispossessed or stripped of my rights. I don't have any. I am an intruder on this story. It doesn't belong to me. But what to do with it, I still don't know, despite our joyfully boozy evenings.

The seasons pass, and we get the most out of them. Line fishing, ice fishing, campfires on the beach, snowshoeing in winter, gathering wood in the fall, suppers at Suzan's. Time flies, companionable and generous. Is there deep inside me the unconscious desire to let it fly? To hold on to my pages so they keep stirring the fire of our evenings? The time I spend in Clova has become precious to me.

But I have to decide to do something with my pages. There are too many of them, I would agree, and as they were written they became too personal for the 'report' Patrice wants me to produce. Desmond is right. They will end up in the wastebasket without being read. Patrice bitches and moans. It has become an obsession. VIA Rail lets old women die; VIA Rail lets its trains die; VIA Rail will let us die by a thousand cuts. We all know that it is his online business he is protecting.

Patrice thinks this story has gone on too long, that I should have sent my 'report' to VIA Rail long ago, that our Transcontinental is increasingly in peril, and that, if the story of the pharaoh's daughter was powerful enough to save baby Moses and Lisana, it could also save the Transcontinental, 'and basta, enough, send in your report.'

Urgency is Patrice's watchword, whereas Desmond insists on the importance of what he calls my 'oeuvre,' a word that makes my skin crawl. He also says 'your novel,' which is no better. It is outrageous, pretentious, grotesque. The humble English teacher, son of a railwayman, and spurned lover will certainly not let a novelist's wings grow. Desmond insists, I resist, we have our little duels, and Suzan smiles in contentment. She likes to watch us argue around her table. She is the one who came up with the idea of the wandering chronicle. The idea is outlandish, she knows it, and she doesn't push it. Too outlandish to discuss seriously, it wasn't something we ever dwelled on for long, but it makes for a pleasant image. A story of roaming on the railway that roams on the railway.

Above us hovers the thinking of my friend Bernie, who follows our discussions from afar. Bernie is at the origin of this chronicle. Astonishingly, he is in no hurry to see it in one form or another. Report, novel, roaming chronicle, none of it matters to him. 'No rush, we can wait.' Wait for what? 'For the loon across the Atlantic to publish his novel.' What's important is that 'Gladys's real story' be safely stored in the memory of my computer and when the time comes that it can stand up to 'the web of lies from that loon.' My chronicle – or whatever you want to call it – is a rampart against the loon's fanciful construction, and it will stand up in all of its truth when the time comes.

The problem is that Léonard Mostin doesn't seem in a rush to finish his novel. On my last visit to Toronto, Lisana had received a postcard from Moscow.

'Moscow, that's far,' Bernie commented, and I saw a smile of satisfaction at knowing that the novelist was thousands of kilometres from his desk.

Are we condemned, Léonard Mostin and me, on either side of the Atlantic, to chase a story without an end?

For the time being, Clova is the centre of the world. Time flies, friendship is precious, and I prefer to sit at Suzan's table or, even better, on her porch.

'Que je sois, que tu sois, qu'il soit, que …'

' … nous soyons, que vous soyez, qu'ils soient.'

'It's so complicated. I don't have enough years left.'

For the time being, Suzan has got it into her head to learn French, and she has a hard time with the subjunctive. When a train goes by, and she settles deep down into her chair, I know that it is a verb conjugation that I see moving on her lips.

'Que je publie, que tu publies, qu'il …'

'I won't publish.'

'Que j'oublie, que tu oublies …'

'I won't forget.'

'Que …'

'That I liberate myself, that I liberate my pages, that I let them take flight …'

' … on one train, then another, and …'

' … and I will have finished my chronicle.'

I will have to explain it to Bernie.

Acknowledgements

From the author
For their support, friendship, and invaluable information throughout my travelling chronicle, I would like to thank:

Chantal Côté, Robert Moreau, Diane Armstrong, Carl Ouimet, Marthe Brown, Claude Chartrand, Nicole Perron, Anne-Marie Perron, Craig Kennet, Danièle Coulombe, Denis Cloutier, Sylviane Martineau, Denis Morin, Bettie Ethier, Nancy Hollmer, Marie Lebel, Julie Langevin, Normand Renaud, Julie Latimer, Bill McLeod, Karen Bachman, David Yaschyshya, Marie Daviau-Aumont, Frederick Bonin, Jean-Pierre Villeneuve, Claude Villeneuve, Renée Lamontagne, Carolyn O'Neil, and, of course, Bernie Jaworsky.

From the translator
Thank you to Alana Wilcox, Coach House Books, and Jocelyne Saucier for waiting. Eternal thanks to Owen Egan, Joni Dufour, and Donna for giving me a place to land.

Jocelyne Saucier's *Il pleuvait des oiseaux* (*And the Birds Rained Down*) garnered her the Prix des cinq continents de la Francophonie, making her the first Canadian to win the award. The book was a CBC Canada Reads Selection in 2015 and its movie adaptation premiered at the Toronto International Film Festival in 2019.

Rhonda Mullins has translated Jocelyne Saucier's two previous novels for Coach House. *And the Birds Rained Down* was a finalist for CBC Canada Reads and the Governor General's Literary Award for Translation. She received the Governor General's Award in 2015 for translating Saucier's *Twenty-One Cardinals*.

Typeset in Jenson Pro and Morison.

Printed at the Coach House on bpNichol Lane in Toronto, Ontario, on
Zephyr Antique Laid paper, which was manufactured, acid-free, in Saint-
Jérôme, Quebec, from second-growth forests. This book was printed with
vegetable-based ink on a 1973 Heidelberg KORD offset litho press. Its pages
were folded on a Baumfolder, gathered by hand, bound on a Sulby Auto-
Minabinda, and trimmed on a Polar single-knife cutter.

Coach House is on the traditional territory of many nations, including the
Mississaugas of the Credit, the Anishnabeg, the Chippewa, the Haudeno-
saunee, and the Wendat peoples, and is now home to many diverse First
Nations, Inuit, and Métis peoples. We acknowledge that Toronto is covered
by Treaty 13 with the Mississaugas of the Credit. We are grateful to live
and work on this land.

Edited by Alana Wilcox
Interior design by Crystal Sikma
Author photo by Ariane Ouellet
Translator photo by Owen Egan

Coach House Books
80 bpNichol Lane
Toronto ON M5S 3J4
Canada

416 979 2217
800 367 6360

mail@chbooks.com
www.chbooks.com